"Did You Have To Say We're Married?"

Victoria wailed.

"What did you expect me to do? You're the one who didn't want to claim me as a relative," Dare reminded her. "Besides, my being your husband is better."

"How on earth do you figure that?"

"Elementary, Teach. It gives me a legitimate excuse to stick close to you, since I can pretend to be hot for your bod. That shouldn't be too hard to do."

"I'm going to forget you said that. And quit calling me *Teach*. It's *Miss Cooper* to you!"

"Not anymore it's not. The way I figure it, we've been married—" Dare consulted his watch "—ten minutes now. Which reminds me. You need to quit calling *me* Marshal. Call me Dare. Or darling."

Dear Reader,

There's so much in store for you this month from Silhouette Desire! First, don't miss *Cowboys Don't Cry* by Anne McAllister. Not only is this a *Man of the Month*— it's also the first book in her CODE OF THE WEST series. Look for the next two books in this series later in the year.

Another terrific miniseries, FROM HERE TO MATERNITY by Elizabeth Bevarly, also begins, with *A Dad Like Daniel*. These delightful stories about the joys of unexpected parenthood continue in April and June!

For those of you who like a touch of the otherworldly, take a look at Judith McWilliams's *Anything's Possible!* And the month is completed by Carol Devine's *A Man of the Land*, Audra Adams's *His Brother's Wife*, and *Truth or Dare* by Caroline Cross.

Next month, we celebrate the 75th *Man of the Month* with a very special Desire title, **That Burke Man** by **Diana Palmer**. It's part of her LONG, TALL TEXANS series, and I know you won't want to miss it!

Happy reading!

Lucia Macro
Senior Editor

Please address questions and book requests to:
Silhouette Reader Service
U.S.: 3010 Walden Ave., P.O. Box 1325, Buffalo, NY 14269
Canadian: P.O. Box 609, Fort Erie, Ont. L2A 5X3

CAROLINE CROSS
CROSS
TRUTH OR DARE

SILHOUETTE *Desire*®
Published by Silhouette Books
America's Publisher of Contemporary Romance

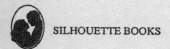

SILHOUETTE BOOKS

ISBN 0-373-05910-8

TRUTH OR DARE

Books by Caroline Cross

Silhouette Desire

Dangerous #810
Rafferty's Angel #851
Truth or Dare #910

CAROLINE CROSS

grew up in eastern Washington state, where she acquired a love of books and horses, long summer days and wide-open spaces. Although she's an inveterate reader, it wasn't until after the birth of her second child that she discovered the magic of contemporary romance fiction. Fascinated by the opportunity to write about what interests her most—people, and why they behave as they do—she began her first book and has been writing ever since. She now lives outside Seattle with her husband, two daughters and an ever-expanding collection of pets.

One

He stood in the shadows, a dull black automatic pistol in his hand.

Victoria slammed to a halt as she stepped across the kitchen threshold. For one endless second of terror, she thought he meant to shoot her. Lord knew he looked dangerous enough, what with the shaggy cut of his thick black hair, two days' growth of beard on his jaw and the cool hard stare of his smoke gray eyes.

Her heart dropped to her knees. The cheerful sound of the neighborhood kids playing Red Rover out in the sunny street vanished, drowned out by the roar of the blood in her ears.

Up until this moment, the events of the past nine weeks hadn't seemed quite real—not the attempt she'd witnessed to plant a bomb in Judge Barnett's suitcase at the Billings airport, or the threat she'd since received warning her not to testify about it. But now...

She clutched the bag of groceries she'd carried in from the car tighter, as if a loaf of bread could save her from a bullet.

Her uninvited visitor tensed at even that slight movement. "You the teacher—Ms. Cooper?" His voice was hard; his smokey eyes were as watchful as a jungle cat's.

For a moment, she was too frightened to think, much less answer. But then, mercifully, recognition dawned. While she didn't own a TV, she did receive several out-of-state newspapers. His face—his lean, handsome, arrogant face—had been splashed all over both the *Washington Post* and the *New York Times* the previous week, she realized. The headlines had been the same: *International Furor As Deputy U.S. Marshal Nabs Colombian Drug Czar. Third World Nations Lodge U.N. Protest.*

U.S. Marshal... "Did—did Mr. McDunna send you?" Malcolm McDunna, the assistant U.S. attorney for Montana, was in charge of the Barnett case.

He gave a slight nod. "That's right." He thumbed the safety on the gun, then shoved it under the waistband of his jeans at the small of his back.

Relief flooded her, making her weak in the knees. She groped for the edge of the counter. "Oh, thank goodness."

"Aw, hell. A fainter." So swiftly she didn't have a chance to protest, he surged across the room, plucked the grocery bag away from her and dumped it on the counter. A split second later, he wrapped one big callused hand around her waist, slid the other beneath her trembling knees and swept her effortlessly into his arms.

"Oh!" He was all rock-solid satin-over-steel heat. Nonplussed—nothing in the rules of decorum Great-Aunt Alice had drummed into her had prepared her for this— Victoria sucked in a breath, then gave a faint gasp as his warm male scent filled her head. Despite the August heat, she shivered. "Oh, please. Put me down!"

He hooked a kitchen chair with one booted foot and dragged it away from the table. "Not until I'm sure I won't have to scrape you up off the floor," he said grimly. His body rippled with power as he settled down with her across his lap.

"Oh, but—"

"Don't you understand English, Teach? *No.*"

It was his vehemence rather than the words that silenced her. Sitting rigidly within the circle of his arms, Victoria squeezed her eyes shut, counted to three and told herself not to panic.

It was easier said than done. Particularly when he was so close she could feel the strong, steady beat of his heart. It was in marked contrast to her own, which was racing as though she'd just dashed uphill for five miles with a pack of demons chasing after her.

Calm down, she told herself. He's a federal agent. A certified good guy who's been sent to protect you.

Oh, yeah? some reckless portion of her brain scoffed. With those chiseled lips and that killer bod? He doesn't look like any law enforcement officer *I've* ever seen. He looks like the kind of man about whom Aunt Alice always warned you. Remember? The kind who sent mothers scurrying to lock up their daughters in previous centuries? The kind it seems pretty obvious it would be wise to avoid in *this* one?

The unkind thought was like a dash of cold water, bringing Victoria up short. Although there had obviously been a mistake—she'd made her situation clear when she'd spoken to Mr. McDunna and he'd promised to send her someone appropriate, which this man most assuredly was not— that still didn't give her cause to assassinate his character, as Aunt Alice had been wont to say.

Besides, he didn't appear crazed or predatory. Just... rough. And despite his dangerous looks and his high-handed manner, if he meant to hurt her, he'd had a clear shot when she walked in the door. But he hadn't. Instead, he'd valiantly leaped to her assistance when he thought she might faint.

Oh, please, said the rebellious little voice in her head. That "valiant" gesture wouldn't have been necessary if he hadn't first scared you out of your wits. And if he's such a paragon of virtue, why are you still sitting on his lap? You're not afraid of him, are you?

Of course not. To prove it, Victoria opened her eyes, only to blink as she found herself gazing straight into the open V of the marshal's white cotton shirt. She stared, mesmerized, at a taut golden wedge of muscle-slabbed chest.

An unfamiliar hollow feeling bloomed in the pit of her stomach. Disconcerted, she averted her gaze and instinctively tried to scoot away, only to freeze when she realized the skirt of her demure white sundress was belled out around her. That meant there was nothing between her backside and his thighs but her thin satin panties and his tight black jeans...

Mortified, she felt heat burn her cheeks.

When she finally got the courage to glance at the marshal, however, he seemed oblivious to her embarrassment—and, thank the stars, the reason for it. Perhaps he really wasn't so bad...

"Well?" he said brusquely. "You feeling better?"

His breath sent a tendril of her pale blond hair sliding free of her chignon. It tumbled down and draped across his brawny forearm; a strange little burst of warmth shot through her at the sight. "I'm...fine." She gathered her wits and her hair, which she tucked behind her ear, and twisted to face her unlikely Sir Galahad. "Thank you for your concern. Mr....?"

His guarded expression was impossible to read. "Kincaid."

"Oh. Well, it was very kind of you, Mr. Kincaid—"

"Marshal."

She took a deep breath and told herself he wasn't trying to be difficult. *He doesn't have to try,* her little voice observed. *He's already perfected it into an art form.*

Victoria suppressed a sigh. She felt the first faint thrum of a headache coming on. "Yes, well, it was very kind of you to assist me. But I . . . I believe I would like to see your badge. And—and I'd like to get up. Please."

Something she couldn't quite define flickered to life in his dark gray eyes. "You sure?"

"Yes."

"All right."

Without another word, he stood.

His precipitous action startled a totally unladylike yelp out of her as she slid the length of his taut, hard thighs before her feet found the floor. Instinctively, she clutched at him for balance; the next thing she knew, his hands skated up her sides, his fingers straddled her back and the heels of his palms came to rest against the swell of her breasts to steady her.

This time, Victoria thought she really *might* faint as, straightaway, her nipples tightened and a coil of shameful awareness twisted to life inside her. The only thing that kept her on her feet was the thought that if she did pass out, it might give *him* some sort of perverse satisfaction.

"Easy." There was a faint but unmistakable edge of amusement in his voice. "You sure you're okay? You seem a little . . . rocky to me."

"I feel fine," she lied.

"Yeah." There was a meaningful pause. "I noticed."

Oh! She stepped back and glared at him. "The badge— please?"

"Sure thing."

Another unwanted shiver went through her as he slowly dropped his hands, the pads of his fingers burning through her dress. Victoria watched warily as he reached into his back pocket, snapped open a battered leather case and dangled it before her eyes. There was a five-pointed silver star inside with a picture ID beside it.

She took her own sweet time examining it, determined to shore up her crumbling composure. Finally, she looked up. "Thank you."

He snapped the case shut. "You're welcome." He shoved it back in his pocket and made a swift survey of the cheerful room with its white counters and cabinets set off by a display of bright blue crockery. He walked to the fridge, opened it and scanned the contents, then flicked a speculative glance at the grocery bag lying on the counter. "I don't suppose there's a beer in there?"

"Beer? Of course not."

"Dumb question," he murmured.

Stung, she said without thinking, "Isn't it against the rules to drink on duty?"

His mouth quirked sardonically. "Now, Teach—do I look like the kind of guy who lies awake at night worrying about the rules?"

Dumb question, she mimicked silently, as he turned back to the fridge, grabbed a can of cola and opened it. She watched the strong, smooth column of his throat work as he took a swig. She wondered at the sudden dryness in her own mouth. What was the matter with her?

More to the point, what was the matter with *him* that he had such a strong effect on her? She'd spent all of fifteen minutes with him and already she was behaving with less maturity than the eighth graders she taught at Gage Primary.

He was just so big, she thought, measuring the width of his shoulders with her eyes as he strode to the screen door. And so vital; he radiated energy the way a furnace generated heat. And he was unarguably striking, if your taste ran to intense, dark-haired men who had clearly taken more than their share of walks on the wild side.

Not that hers did, she amended hastily, reining in her thoughts. If anything, his overwhelming virility was simply another reason why this would never work. In a town as small as Gage, an unmarried schoolteacher was expected to comport herself in an exemplary way. As she'd explained to Mr. McDunna, she had a certain reputation to maintain. There was no way she could spend the next two weeks living with a man—particularly one as brash as this one—without destroying it. She had to do something.

She cleared her throat. "I'm afraid there's been a mistake."

He made a sound that could only be described as a snort and turned from the door. "Tell me about it, Teach. As far as I can see, you don't need a bodyguard. You need a keeper."

She stared at him, taken aback by his unexpected attack. "What does that mean?"

"Think about it. What the hell would you have done if I'd been the guy who's threatening you?"

She thought about the terror and helplessness she'd felt when she'd walked in the door and found him standing there. He was right, she realized. She hadn't acted very wisely. She should have run, screamed, done *something*. At the very least, she should have had the sense not to just barge in.

But she wasn't about to admit it. Not to him. Every instinct she possessed told her that if she gave this man an inch, he'd take the entire yardstick. "I could have defended myself."

One dark eyebrow rose. "Oh, yeah? What did you have planned? To off the creep with a loaf of bread?"

She flushed. "I would've thought of something."

"Right. Didn't McDunna tell you to stay put until someone could get here?"

Victoria shook her head. "No, he did not."

He gave her a long look over the soft drink can. "What exactly *did* he say?"

"Not much of anything," she said stiffly. "As a matter of fact, when I called last week to tell him I'd received a threat, he didn't seem concerned at all. He said that sort of intimidation was unusual for the group responsible for trying to plant the bomb in the judge's suitcase. That, as it wasn't their normal style, he deemed it unlikely they'd follow through, and so I shouldn't worry."

"Easy for him to say," Kincaid muttered, his disgust obvious. "He's not the one risking his neck. What other jewels of wisdom did he pass along?"

"Well . . . none really. He was very brisk when he called back yesterday. He told me that after a review of the case, it had been decided I did need protection and that someone would be here today. But he didn't say a word about me not going anywhere. Much less—" she turned to keep the marshal in view as he paced restlessly across the room "—anything that led me to expect to be treated like . . . this."

Kincaid swiveled around. "Like what?"

She looked at him in disbelief. "Oh, for heaven's sake. Like breaking into my house and scaring me half to death, that's what."

He looked at her intently. "I scared you?" When she nodded, he gave a satisfied grunt. "Good."

She gaped at him. *"Good?"*

"That's right." His gaze dropped briefly to her parted lips, then bounced back up to her eyes. "You ought to be scared, lady. It's a helluva motivator when it comes to staying alive. God knows, from what I've seen so far, you can use all the help you can get. I've only done a preliminary check, but it was enough to show me your security stinks. Your windows don't have screens and most of the latches don't work, including the one in your bedroom. An anemic twelve-year-old armed with a putty knife could jimmy either of your doors. Of course—" he made no effort to hide his sarcasm "—that's provided you bothered to stay home and lock them first. Hell. You might as well put a neon sign out front and declare it open season on dinky little blue-eyed blondes."

"You were in my bedroom?" For some reason, the thought of him invading her private, personal space was far more upsetting than the rest of his criticism. Particularly when she remembered the basket of clean laundry she'd left sitting beside her dresser, her lingerie on top. Of course, there was always the chance he hadn't noticed the contents....

For half a second, his face seemed to soften as he registered her distress. But then his rain-colored gaze again strayed to her mouth and something he saw there appeared to annoy him.

His expression hardened. He lifted his eyes, and his look became calculated. "That's right. I've gotta say—you surprise me, Teach. Nice undies. I especially like the peekaboo red ones with the black lace."

Oh! Who was she trying to kid? He might be with the government but he was definitely *not* nice. He was insufferably arrogant and terribly rude and—

And, if she let him, it was clear he would turn her peaceful, well-ordered life on its ear in the course of a single afternoon. A peace and a life she'd worked hard to achieve. Her chin came up. "I'm sorry," she said with patent insincerity. "But this simply isn't going to work. I think—I think it would be best if you leave."

He crossed his arms across his chest and rocked back on his heels. "Don't I wish. But unfortunately—for both of us—we're stuck with each other."

"Hardly. I'll just call Mr. McDunna and explain—"

"He's on vacation."

"Then I'll talk to whomever is in charge!"

"Be my guest. But it isn't going to do you any good. Trust me. Do you think I *volunteered* to come here?"

She added odious to her list of his unflattering attributes. "You don't understand. Mr. McDunna promised me a female agent. Or someone older. Lots older. As I told him, this is a small town. Even when I explain why you're here, there's going to be a certain amount of speculation about the time we spend alone together and—"

"No," he said flatly. "There isn't."

"Marshal Kincaid," she said a little desperately, "you obviously don't understand how small towns work—"

"Maybe not. But I understand enough to know I'm not going to broadcast my presence to the nut case who sent you that note."

"But then, what—" She stopped and stared at him, appalled. "Are you suggesting we lie?"

"That's right, Teach. You can say I'm your cousin, or something."

"But both my parents were only children and everyone in town knows it! And even if they didn't..." She thought about the way her hormones tried to seize control from her brain whenever he got too close and knew there was no way she could convince anyone she regarded him as a cousin. "Even if they didn't, I—I still couldn't."

"You can. And you will."

Their gazes clashed, gray eyes locked with blue.

"No. I won't." A second passed. Then two. The only sound in the kitchen was the faint ticking of the clock and the rasp of their breathing.

Victoria was darned if she was going to be the first to look away. Yet, as the moments stretched out, it got harder and harder to ignore certain other things.

Such as how exotic he looked, with his shining black hair and beard-shadowed cheeks.

And how powerful he was, from the strong, chiseled bones of his face to the sleek solid muscle in his arms, chest and legs.

And how strange she was beginning to feel. Hot. And breathless. As if the temperature had risen ten degrees. As if there weren't enough air in the room for both of them—

A knock at the door jerked her around. Victoria suppressed a groan as she saw her neighbor, Mrs. Vonnegut, standing there, a look of avid curiosity on her round little face. The elderly woman might be a dear, but she was also an inveterate gossip.

In the way of small towns everywhere, Mrs. Vonnegut didn't wait for an invitation but pulled open the screen and bustled inside, a cloth-covered pie plate in her hand. "Hello, dear," she said brightly. "I saw your friend arrive on his motorcycle. When he put it in the shed, I took it to mean he was staying for a while, so I thought you might want to offer him a nice piece of pie—for dessert, after dinner? Since I well recall how dear, dear Alice despaired of your ever learning to bake, and since I happened to make an extra, why, I decided I'd just run this right over. It's blueberry." Mrs. Vonnegut sucked in a much-needed breath and dumped her fragrant offering on the counter. Smiling benignly, she locked her gaze on Victoria's visitor as if it were the targeting mechanism on a heat-seeking missile.

Victoria took a deep breath of her own and smiled back, wondering what else could go wrong. "That's very kind of you, Doris, but—"

"Now, dear. Where are your manners? Aren't you going to introduce us?"

The sensitive skin on the back of Victoria's neck tingled as the marshal stepped up beside her. "Well, I—" she started to answer, only to stop in shock when he hooked an arm around her shoulders and pulled her close.

"Dare Kincaid, ma'am."

Dare? She might have known, Victoria thought a little wildly, suddenly unable to breathe at all.

Mrs. Vonnegut's eyes widened at their intimate stance. "I . . . see." She shifted her gaze to Victoria, her expression accusing. "I didn't know you had a boyfriend, dear."

"Oh, but I don't—"

"That's right," the man at her side interjected. He tugged Victoria even closer and gave her a warning squeeze. "She doesn't."

The elderly woman's eyebrows knit in confusion. "Then who are you, young man?"

The marshal gave a low, intimate laugh. "Me? Why, I'm Victoria's husband."

TWO

The crack of the screen door rolled through the kitchen like a burst of thunder, signaling Mrs. Vonnegut's departure.

In the silence that followed, Dare braced for a storm.

He didn't have long to wait as Ms. Cooper gave an eloquent shudder, then jerked away from his encircling arm. She turned on him, her big blue eyes charged with a mixture of outrage and dismay. "Oh! Are you out of your mind? How could you!"

His expression impassive, Dare stared back. Why the hell did the woman have to be so damn... teacherish? She was just a little thing, and although she was too uptight for his taste, she wasn't actually bad-looking—despite that voluminous white dress and her old-fashioned hairdo. As a matter of fact, with those eyes and that baby-fine skin, he would've pegged her as at least five years younger than the thirty it said she was in the file.

But the way she held herself—chin up, her little spine as straight as a steel curtain rod—was, unfortunately, all classic, prissy teacher. So was the way she had of pinning him with her gaze. Somehow, she managed to give the impression she was looking down her nose at him, which was ridiculous when he towered over her by at least a foot. Still, it had the intended effect. It made him feel as if he were still the rebel he'd been as a kid.

Not that it mattered, he reminded himself.

Because he *wasn't* that wild Kincaid kid anymore, that bad boy who was always on the edge of trouble. He was a deputy U.S. marshal, and he was here to do a job, whether he—or she—liked it or not.

The sooner Ms. Cooper understood that, the better off they'd both be.

To that end, he hardened himself against her distress and said stonily, "I'm here to protect you, Teach. I'll do whatever it takes to achieve it."

"But did you have to say we're *married?*" she wailed. "And to Doris? It'll be all over town faster than a bad case of flu."

He bit off an exasperated curse. "What did you expect me to do? You're the one who didn't want to claim me as a relative. Remember?"

"Yes, but—"

"Besides, my being your husband is better."

Her jaw dropped momentarily. "How on earth do you figure that?"

"Elementary, Teach. It gives me a legitimate excuse to stick close to you, since I can pretend to be hot for your bod. That shouldn't be too hard to do. I figure if I need some inspiration, I can always think about your racy underwear collection."

She gave him the sort of look he would've expected if he'd reached out and goosed her. "I'm going to try and forget you said that." She enunciated each word as if she were getting paid by the syllable. "And quit calling me Teach. It's *Miss Cooper* to you!"

"Not anymore it's not." To his surprise, he realized he actually enjoyed seeing how fast he could make her cheeks turn pink. Not that it was much of a challenge, since everything he said seemed to set her off. "The way I figure it, we've been married—" he consulted his watch "—ten minutes now. That means I can call you pretty much whatever I want. Which reminds me. We'll have to do something about a ring. And *you* need to quit calling *me* Marshal. Call me Dare. Or darling."

She squeezed her eyes shut; her lips worked soundlessly as she appeared to count to twenty before her lashes fluttered up.

She tried a different tack. "Don't you understand?" Her tone was earnest, pitched low in an obvious appeal to his reason. "I can't perpetuate this kind of hoax on my friends and neighbors. It . . . it wouldn't be honest."

"Tough," he said flatly. "Better dishonest and alive than honest and dead."

Those little flags of color were back in her cheeks, but she managed to hold on to her measured tone. "All right, Marshal. Since you have all the answers, how do you propose I explain your sudden absence when this is over?"

"Hell, that's easy. By then you can tell the truth."

"Oh, for— Obviously, you weren't paying attention earlier."

He gave her a cynical look. "You mean that stuff about your reputation?"

"No! I mean that 'stuff' about your not understanding small towns. What you're proposing is the same as a vote of no confidence. It's saying I don't trust my friends and neighbors—"

"Hell, no, lady. It's saying *I* don't trust them—and I don't!"

"Yes, but you're not the one who lives here—"

He raised a placating hand, gesturing her to silence. "Okay. You're right. So forget the truth. Lie. Claim you married me in a fit of passion, but after we lived together awhile, you realized you'd made a mistake.''

She rolled her eyes. "Oh, that's a great suggestion! I teach eighth grade. Do you have any idea the kind of example that sets for my students?''

She was doing *it* again, giving him that superior, down-the-nose teacher look. Annoyed, Dare pretended to think, then leaned forward and said in a soft, silky voice, "All right. Say I seemed like a nice guy at first—until you learned the shocking truth. That I wanted you. Anytime. Anywhere. Anyplace. That I was insatiable, that I was after you to do all sorts of lewd, improper things, and you, being a true paragon of virtue, were revolted. Just think. Even if you don't have everyone's sympathy, at least you'll have their envy—''

She stared at him, her eyes wide with disbelief. "Oh! That's it! You obviously refuse to take this seriously!'' Turning on her heel, she marched toward the phone that hung above the counter next to the door into the hall. "I'm going to call Mr. McDunna and get this straightened out. Now. Before it gets any worse.'' Consulting a piece of paper, she began to punch a series of numbers into the phone.

Dare considered telling her it wouldn't do any good, then said to hell with it as he realized he'd done just that, earlier. "Go ahead. It's your nickel. I'll just fix myself something to eat.''

She turned and glared at him. "No! Absolutely not! You stay out of my drawers!''

This was like shooting fish in a barrel. He gave her a quick look up and down, raised one eyebrow, and she flushed to the roots of her hair.

"I mean... That is... I— *Hello?*'' Lowering her voice, she whirled, turning her back on him in a belated attempt to reclaim her dignity. She pressed the receiver to her ear. "Malcolm McDunna, please.'' A pause. Then, "What?

What do you mean he's *gone? Gone* where? For how long?"

Feeling magnanimous, Dare quelled the urge to say "I told you so." Instead, he pulled the loaf of bread from the sack on the counter and began to rummage through the cupboards.

He was behaving badly, he knew, but he couldn't seem to help it. There was just something about Miss Too-Good-To-Be-True Cooper that brought out the worst in him. Maybe it was her invisible-book-on-the-head posture or her old-fashioned air of naiveté or simply that "teacher" look, but she made him feel as itchy and restless as an eight-year-old boy forced to don a starched shirt and his Sunday-school suit. Put simply, she annoyed the hell out him.

So did her big old rambling neo-Victorian house. Situated as it was, on a large lot on a tree-lined street among similar houses, with high ceilings, lots of windows and a big wraparound porch, he supposed some people might find it charming. He, however, thought it looked better suited to Mayberry than Bonanza, and wondered who the hell had thought to build such a thing in Montana. Bottom line was, the thing was going to be a sonofagun to secure, and he wasn't looking forward to it.

Of course, a small portion of his irritation might stem from his being tired, he acknowledged grudgingly. He hadn't had more than a handful of hours' sleep in the past week. He'd flown more than sixty-five hundred air miles, crossed three time zones, five foreign countries and eight states. He'd met with the press. He'd even been debriefed twice, once in Miami and again in D.C.

Given those facts, it wasn't surprising that while his body might be here, his mind was having a hard time making the necessary leap from slimy drug dealers to endangered American schoolmarms.

I never should have told Arizzo to shove it when he suggested I take a vacation, he reflected, setting a jar of dill pickles on the counter next to the peanut butter. If I'd been paying better attention and not been so pissed off about the uproar over Mendelez's arrest, I would've realized the old man was trying to get me to lay low. And if I'd just had the sense to keep my mouth shut, right now I'd be lolling on a white sand beach with some adoring, dark-eyed beauty in a string bikini, instead of baby-sitting a pint-size teacher with an attitude.

But then, the last thing he'd expected when he refused to take time off was that his boss would assign him to a witness security job. Hell, why should he have? Hadn't Dare single-handedly brought in three fugitives on the Marshals Fifteen Most Wanted list in twenty-two months? Damn straight, he had.

Unfortunately, Arizzo hadn't been too happy about Dare's methods. "You've got to quit acting as if you're a one-man strike force," the older man had said acidly after they'd concluded the formal debriefing. "You're just damn lucky this last little caper didn't blow up in your face. What did you think you were doing, pretending to be the damn steward on that charter flight? And taking off without a backup, I might add? Hell, the way you let things go so late, we were damn lucky we had enough time to let the Bahamian authorities know you were coming! What the devil would you have done if they'd refused to let you land? Huh, hotshot?"

"Ah, come on, Mike," Dare had scoffed, unwilling to admit the truth of what the chief deputy was saying. "It wasn't my fault there were some last-minute changes. I did the best I could, given the situation. Have some faith—I was on top of it all the way."

Arizzo had wagged a finger under Dare's nose. "Don't b.s. me, Kincaid. You got lucky. If Mendelez had caught on, you would have come home in a coffin."

"Maybe. But I would've brought him with me."

"Damn it! It's that kind of attitude I'm talking about!" Arizzo had shouted.

Gazes locked, the two men had stared belligerently at each other for several long seconds.

And then, unexpectedly, Arizzo's pale eyes had softened. "Listen," he'd said in a more subdued voice, "nobody's sorrier than me that Jimmy died. He was a good man. But it's over and done with. He's gone, and all the grandstanding in the world isn't going to bring him back. I know for a fact Falwell's been after you to teach at FLETC. You ought to say yes—while you're still alive to do it."

When Dare had said nothing, simply sat, his jaw set, his expression guarded, Arizzo had sighed. "Fine then, you pigheaded jackass. But at least take some time off. Hell, according to your file, you haven't taken more than a day here and there since before the shooting. You're way overdue for a vacation."

That was when Dare had blown it. Guilt-ridden and on edge the way he always was when the incident that had taken his best friend's life came up, he'd lashed out and told Arizzo what he could do with his vacation.

He swore under his breath, remembering. *Dammit, Jimmy. It's been three years since you went and got yourself killed and you're still getting me in trouble.*

Despite the black humor, the thought was accompanied by a grinding sense of remorse that always occurred when he let himself think about his late partner.

Well, hell. That was good, he told himself, as he checked the label on a jar and discovered it was jelly, gave a grunt of satisfaction and set it next to the pickles. The memory of what had happened to Jimmy—what he'd *allowed* to happen to Jimmy—was a forceful reminder of what was at stake here. Although he had a strong hunch Ms. Cooper wasn't actually in any danger, that this assignment was nothing but a red herring designed by his boss to get *him* out of the spotlight and see to it he got some rest, it wasn't a theory he cared to test. He wasn't taking any chances with the school-teacher's life.

Nope. They were going to do this one by the book.

No friendship, no fraternization, no Kodak moments, no warm-and-fuzzy stuff.

No one who mattered to him lying dead in a pool of blood when it was over—

He slammed the door on the thought. Firmly setting his mind on the matter at hand, he put together his sandwich, arranged it, a pickle and some chips on a plate and plunked down at the table just as Victoria hung up.

Her slender shoulders, pale gold against the virginal white of her dress, were bowed with defeat.

"No luck, huh?" he said around a mouthful of sandwich.

She turned at the sound of his voice. Her lower lip quivered; she caught it in her teeth. Once she had things under control, she took a deep breath and cleared her throat. To her credit, she met his gaze squarely. "No. You were right. Mr. McDunna is unavailable and his assistant doesn't have any authority over the witness protection assignments."

He took another bite and didn't comment, only watched as she slowly approached and sat down in the chair opposite him.

"So what do we do now?" she asked, her voice subdued as she gazed blankly at the table. Her thick, dusky lashes cast a faint shadow on her smooth face while a silky tendril of hair, the color of early-morning sunshine, tickled against the delicate curve of her cheek.

He studied her, startled by the sudden tightness in his chest. With a scowl, he decided it was her air of defeat that was bothering him. It didn't have one damn thing to do with the gentle swell of her breasts beneath that old-maid dress or the kitten-soft look of vulnerability on her face. "*We* don't do anything," he growled, tossing his half-eaten sandwich on his plate.

Startled, she looked up, then raised her chin defensively at his caustic expression. "Well, pardon me. I assume you have some point you want to make?"

He stretched out his legs, folded his hands across his middle and rocked back so the chair was balanced on two legs. "As a matter of fact, I do. It's this—I lay down the rules. You shut up, listen and do precisely what I say."

Her expressive face registered her dismay. But to his surprise, she didn't immediately object. Instead, she thought about it before she said slowly, "I . . . see. And what exactly are your . . . rules?"

"To start?" He ticked off the items on his fingers. "I answer the phone. I answer the door. I get the mail. Nobody comes in unless I say so. You don't go out without me. If you're not certain about something, if there's someone you want to see or something you need to do, you clear it with me first."

"But that's—that's . . ." She shook her head, at a temporary loss for words. "No. I'm sorry, Marshal, but I can't. I *won't*. I'm not some child you can order around."

His mouth curved humorlessly. "Dare, sweetheart, remember? And yes, as I believe I said earlier—you can and you will."

Her chin rose again. "I'd like to know how you propose to make me."

He steepled his hands together and looked at her over the top. "Simple. Either you do things my way or *I'll* make a phone call and we'll see how you like being locked up as a material witness."

"You can't do that!"

He sent her a steely, unwavering look.

Her eyes widened. "Can you?"

For the first time since she'd walked in and discovered him planted in her kitchen like the bad seed, he smiled.

It was a cool, calculated, utterly ruthless smile. "Care to find out?"

Just as he figured, it didn't take more than half a second for her to decide she didn't.

They ate in the dining room that night. Dark and gloomy, with formal maroon and cream-colored wallpaper, an ancient Persian rug and oversize mahogany furniture, it was a room that Victoria normally avoided.

Tonight, however, was different. Tonight, the room's funereal air seemed perfectly suited to the oppressive silence that had sprung up between her and the marshal.

Your tax dollars at work, she thought glumly, sneaking a peek at her dinner companion out of the corner of her eye. According to the encyclopedia she'd consulted, there were about twenty-nine hundred deputy U.S. marshals spread out across the United States. Yet who had they sent her? Someone boyishly charming like Tom Cruise? Someone virile but approachable like Harrison Ford? Someone steady and reassuring like Tom Skerritt?

Good heavens, no. She'd been stuck with a street-smart Billy Ray Cyrus doing a Dirty Harry impression.

She quelled an urge to sigh.

In all fairness, she supposed his antisocial attitude might have something to do with the quality of the meal. While Aunt Alice had been a whiz in the kitchen, Victoria had no illusions about her own culinary abilities. On a good day, she'd been known to burn soup—and tonight she'd been understandably distracted. As a result, she'd scorched the rolls, mistakenly added bean with bacon soup to the tuna casserole and done something to the gelatin that had resulted in its failure to fully set up, compelling her to serve it in water glasses.

To his credit, the marshal had yet to say a word. But then, he hadn't said much of anything since she'd agreed to do things his way. Not that he'd gloated; he'd simply kept to himself. After her capitulation, he'd gone out to the shed, toted in a pair of black leather saddlebags and appropriated the big bedroom at the top of the stairs. Once settled—how long, after all, did it take to unpack saddlebags?—he'd checked out the grounds and taken a second, unhurried tour of the interior of the house, making notes as he measured windows and doors and tested locks.

Now, here they were. Victoria knew she should be grateful for his silence, that she ought to thank her lucky stars that he wasn't issuing more rules, restrictions and regulations.

But the truth was, it felt strange to have a man in the house and she longed for a little friendly conversation to ease the strain. Aunt Alice had been a dedicated maiden lady of sixty when she agreed to take in her four-year-old great-niece. Accustomed to a quiet, genteel life-style, she hadn't approved of men on general principle—a sentiment that had included Max Cooper, the brash young Air Force pilot who'd married her only niece.

Nor had Victoria's father made any effort to redeem himself in the elderly lady's eyes. Although his visits had been the highlight of Victoria's childhood, they'd been sporadic and had never lasted more than a few hours. While Victoria could vividly recall the thrill of anticipating his arrival, she could also remember the crushing disappointment when he wouldn't show up—and Aunt Alice's not-so-subtle reminders that it was his wild, irresponsible Cooper blood that was responsible for his behavior and her disappointment. Although the elderly lady had been far too principled to ever acknowledge it outright, Victoria had long suspected that Aunt Alice had been secretly relieved when her nephew-in-law crashed his A-6 into a mountainside. At least that way, he'd no longer been around to be an unsuitable influence in his daughter's life.

Dare laid down his fork with a click, jarring her from her thoughts. "There are some things we need to discuss."

She was instantly on guard. So far, every time they had a "discussion," he came out ahead. "Such as?"

"Let's start with you telling me what happened in Billings."

She didn't bother to try to hide her surprise. "Don't you know?"

He shrugged his broad shoulders. "I've read the report. But I'd like to hear it from you. It'll give me a better feel for what went down." Sprawled in his chair, arms folded across his chest, he was the picture of indifference. Except for the expression in his eyes, which was dead serious.

"Oh. Well..." She gathered her thoughts. "There's not much to tell. Where do you want me to start?"

"Try the beginning," he suggested politely.

Stung by his patronizing tone, for one mad moment she was tempted to do exactly that, just to see if she could wipe that superior look from his face.

She tried to imagine it. "Well, you see, Marshal," she pictured herself saying, "I turned thirty in May. One morning I got up, looked in the mirror and decided that life was passing me by. I guess I went a little crazy. First I threw out all my practical cotton panties and bought silk G-strings and satin bikinis. Then I spent two months' salary on a ten-day cruise. Unfortunately, instead of the wild, tempestuous shipboard romance I'd hoped for, I found myself on a boat booked almost exclusively by the Golden Age Retirement Club. After six days of Parcheesi, shuffleboard and numerous conversations about the merits of assorted dental fixatives, I jumped ship, only to wind up an unwitting witness to a bungled murder attempt."

It would almost be worth sacrificing her pride to see his reaction.

Victoria swallowed a sigh. Almost—but not quite.

She folded her napkin and laid it next to her plate, her movements calm and deliberate, the result of Aunt Alice's lessons on proper deportment. "I was on my way home from vacation. The flight was delayed in Miami and was late arriving in Billings. By the time the luggage finally came off the plane, everyone was tired, impatient and in a hurry. Things were chaotic. When they calmed down and the crowd cleared out, the man who'd been my seatmate on the plane was missing his bag. He wasn't feeling very well, so I offered to go inquire about it while he stayed put, just in case his bag did turn up.

"I was tired, too, and unfamiliar with the Billings airport. I took a wrong turn and wound up in a restricted area, where I spotted a man in coveralls. He was kneeling on the floor beside a luggage cart. Naturally, I assumed he worked for the airline, so I stopped and asked directions.

"He took one look at me and got this funny look on his face. That's when I noticed he was wrestling with a package caught on the zipper of a partially opened bag. The bag was a black-on-black tapestry one, very distinctive—just like the one my acquaintance back at the luggage carousel had just described to me."

She shrugged. "Instinct took over, I guess. I pretended I hadn't noticed anything amiss and asked for directions to the ticket counter. The man mumbled something, I thanked him, went back the way I'd come and notified airport security. That's it."

Dare took his time digesting what she'd said, and then gave her a look that was impossible to interpret. "A lot of people would've preferred not to get involved," he said after a moment. "They would've shrugged it off and convinced themselves it was all a coincidence."

Victoria shook her head. "Oh, I don't think so. Don't forget, I didn't know then that my seatmate was a federal judge, so it never crossed my mind that the man in the coveralls might have a bomb. I assumed he was a thief, that he was trying to get that package out of the bag, not *in*."

"Yeah." He gave her another of those inscrutable looks. "That's what I mean."

"I'm sure anyone else would've done the same," she said earnestly. "I didn't do anything special. I teach my students that we each have certain obligations as citizens. I certainly couldn't ignore mine."

"Somehow I figured that."

Victoria sat up a little straighter, pricked by his jaded tone, which stated clearly he thought she was hopelessly naive.

"So." He leaned back in his chair, clasped his hands at the back of his neck and stretched his legs. "How did you feel when you got the threat in the mail?"

"What do you mean?"

He shifted impatiently. "Weren't you alarmed?"

"Of course I was."

"Didn't it occur to you to maybe regret that you'd gotten involved?"

"Perhaps—for a moment," she said honestly. "But, as I believe I told you, Mr. McDunna was quite reassuring. And the note itself was so...nicely done. I—I still find it hard to believe that the person who wrote it seriously wishes me harm."

"Really?" He tipped his head to one side. "Why?"

Victoria considered, thinking aloud. "I guess I always thought something of that nature had to come on notebook paper with the message cut from magazine print. You know—the way they always are on TV and in the movies? Mine, however, came on one of those generic fold-over notes with the little gold seals. There was a tasteful blue border and it was neatly printed, in ink, with no misspellings or profanity. It was...succinct. It said BACK OFF— OR ELSE. One of the most difficult writing skills to teach is the ability to be clear and concise," she explained, concentrating on the mundane in an attempt to forget the icy dread that had clutched at her when she'd realized she was being threatened.

Silence. And then the marshal surged to his feet. "Jeez, lady, are you for real?" He shoved a hand through his hair as he paced away. "It was a threat, not a term paper!"

Taken aback, Victoria flushed, suddenly realizing how she must sound—the ultimate old-maid schoolteacher, so out of touch with reality, she didn't have a shred of common sense.

Yet that wasn't the case at all, she thought in self-defense. On the contrary; even before that paralyzing moment of terror, back when she'd confronted that seedy little man in the hallway of the Billings airport, she'd known there was a risk involved with doing the right thing.

It was just . . . none of it had seemed very real. After all, not once had she been confronted by any actual violence. Why, until this afternoon, she'd never seen anyone with a gun.

But then, today, everything had changed. And the man pacing across her dining room like a caged tiger was the reason for it.

Although the incident hadn't been reported locally, she'd surreptitiously skimmed the previous week's issues of the *New York Times* while making dinner until she'd found the article she'd seen before. It had confirmed that he was indeed the very same marshal who'd arrested Jose Mendelez, a convicted felon who'd walked away from a minimum security prison in Upstate New York four years ago and had since become a major player in the Colombian cocaine trade.

The details were sketchy, reputedly to protect the civilians involved, but somehow Kincaid had arranged to be on a special charter flight taking Mendelez from Honduras to Cuba, neither of which tended to honor extradition requests from the U.S. When the flight had mysteriously wound up in the far more cooperative Grand Bahamas, there had been howls of outrage from several Third World countries, charging that Kincaid had "helped" the flight crew navigate at gunpoint. Although the allegations had been flatly denied by both the Marshals Service and the State Department, no one was denying that Mendelez's associates had promised to pay a sizable amount for the deputy marshal's head if he ever ventured south of the border again.

The man obviously thrived on dangerous situations. Which, while comforting from the standpoint that he could undoubtedly handle anything, also meant that her own situation must be more serious than she'd been led to believe. Logic dictated the Marshals Service wouldn't send someone like him to protect her unless they were genuinely concerned for her safety.

While Victoria recognized she might be a touch naive, she wasn't stupid.

Consequently, she was scared.

Still, she refused to be a prisoner to it. She'd spent too many years under Aunt Alice's well-meaning but heavy thumb to let anything or anyone dictate to her again. She'd do what the marshal told her—within reason—since it would be foolish not to when his goal was to keep her alive. But—she automatically straightened her spine—she wasn't about to let him tyrannize her. Regardless of what he thought, this was still a free country.

Of course, she didn't think she'd mention it right now.

She looked up and found him standing with his hands on his hips, studying her. He raised one dark eyebrow. "Well? Is that it? Is that all you have to say about being threatened?"

She folded her hands. "Yes. Yes, it is," she said firmly.

His eyes narrowed, but to her surprise, he let it go. He walked over and dropped into his chair. "All right." He picked up his fork, then looked at the food on his plate and set it back down, trying manfully to suppress a shudder. "So...what's your usual routine? Do you have an incredibly busy social life that having a husband is going to disrupt?" For once there was no hint of mockery in his tone.

Perplexed by his unpredictable moods, she said cautiously, "No. I have a student I tutor. Other than that, all I have planned is to work on my lesson plans and get my classroom ready for the coming school year. Oh, and I believe I'm scheduled to work an evening next week at the town health clinic."

"Cancel it."

"But—" She stopped, reminding herself she'd decided to cooperate with him. It shouldn't be too hard to find a replacement, and it might be wise to save her arguments for issues that really mattered. Instinct told her that there were bound to be a few of them. "All right."

"So tell me about this kid you tutor."

"What about him?"

"How old is he, how long have you known him, how often do you see him—and where?"

Victoria considered her answer, and decided that in this case, the less said was probably the better. "His name is Charlie Wells. He's fourteen. We meet here, on Tuesdays and Thursdays."

"So why does he need special help? Is he slow?"

"Absolutely not." One of Kincaid's eyebrows shot up and she could have kicked herself for her defensive tone. This was clearly not the time to bring up Charlie's checkered past. Willing herself to remain calm, she added with feigned nonchalance, "He had a problem that resulted in his missing some school."

He cocked his head. "What sort of problem?"

Victoria's mind raced. "Transportation," she said finally, crossing her fingers under the table to ward off Aunt Alice's ghostly disapproval at such a...creative rendition of the truth. "But it's all taken care of now." She hesitated. "My seeing him isn't going to be a problem, is it?"

He studied her, as if trying to see beyond her calm facade, then stacked his glass and silverware on his plate and stood up. "I don't know yet. For the moment, it's probably best to try and keep up normal appearances. I'll make a final decision after I meet the kid." He gave her another long, penetrating look. "Just don't forget rule number two, Teach."

Victoria gathered up her own dinnerware. "Of course I won't," she said briskly, in a voice that suggested he was crazy for even suggesting such a thing.

Not for her life would she admit that she hadn't the foggiest idea to which rule he was referring.

Three

Maybe there was something to be said for small-town living, after all, Dare decided, as he stood on Victoria's back porch a little past nine the next morning.

He surveyed the assortment of tools and supplies he'd ordered from the local hardware store. He still found it hard to believe they'd been willing to take his order over the phone and then deliver it, free of charge. Yet the proof was right in front of him. All he'd had to do was mention Victoria's name and they'd been happy to accommodate him.

He picked up a hammer and swung it from side to side to test its balance. The thing was top of the line, with a rubberized grip that felt cool against his palm and a solid steel shaft precisely weighted to maximize the thrust of the gleaming metal head. Added to the two dozen other items stacked by the house, which ranged from a level to an electric drill to an assortment of door and window locks, the total for his purchases had come to a small fortune. Arizzo was going to have a conniption fit when Dare turned in his expense account.

The thought helped cheer him a little. Lord knew, he needed all the help he could get; he was still feeling a little off kilter after his dinner conversation with Victoria last night.

He didn't think he'd ever met anyone quite like her. While over the years he'd been willing to buy into the idea that there were still some good, law-abiding, idealistic citizens left, until now he'd personally never met one. His childhood could best be described as rough, and deputy U.S. marshals didn't exactly mix with the cream of society.

Unlike other branches of law enforcement whose members had contact with the innocent as well as the guilty, marshals dealt almost exclusively with convicted felons, people already proven to be on the wrong side of the law, or with criminal informants, people willing to give up their colleagues for personal gain. Since they didn't rescue cats from trees or retrieve little old ladies' handbags or investigate anything other than fugitives' whereabouts, they tended to get a slightly skewed view of the world.

Maybe that explained why he felt as if he'd been dropped into Leave It To Beaverland without a map, he decided, as he began to pop the hinge pins out of the screen door.

Shaking his head, he lifted the screen door from place, carried it across the porch and leaned it up against the railing, where it was safely out of his way. Then he recrossed the porch, stepped inside the house and began removing the pins from the Dutch door.

The sound of a door swinging open snagged his attention. He looked over to see Mrs. Vonnegut bustle out onto her porch. "Yoo-hoo!" She waved. "Good morning, Mr. Kincaid!"

Dare gave a reluctant wave back and tried to look busy, only to stifle a groan when a quick glance showed him the elderly lady wasn't the least put off. Her face set in a determined smile, she swarmed down the stairs and made a bee-line toward him.

He bit off a curse as the gate in the fence between the two properties flew open and she barreled through. "My, my, aren't you the busy one," she exclaimed cheerfully as she marched up the steps. She surveyed the clutter on the porch. "It certainly looks as if you intend to make some improvements around here."

"Yeah. I do." *And one of the first is going to be to nail that gate shut.*

"I'm so glad Victoria has finally found someone to look after her. Such a nice girl. So reliable. I'll never forget how she canceled her plans to go to Paris when her Aunt Alice—"

"Wait a minute," Dare interrupted. "Victoria's aunt's name was Alice . . . Cooper?"

"Oh, no, dear. Alice Bergstrom," Mrs. Vonnegut replied, the significance of his question completely passing her by. "Alice raised Victoria's mother, Lisa, who shocked the town when she ran off with Max Cooper when she was barely eighteen. Alice nearly went out of her mind with worry, only to have her worst fears come true when Lisa was later killed in a car accident. I'm afraid Alice never forgave Max, even though he gave her Victoria to raise. Victoria has always been such a sweet little thing. So even-tempered and biddable. Not like her mother."

She sucked in a much needed breath. "Why, when Alice first got sick, just as dear Victoria was all set to teach at that hoity-toity French school, the dear girl never hesitated. She simply told those highbrow foreigners she couldn't leave her aunt and took a good American job right here in Gage. Of course, poor Alice managed to hang on for years, but I never heard Victoria complain. Such a loyal, steady girl. Dependable, don't you know."

He tried to decide what was more surprising. The news that Ms. Cooper had once planned to live in Paris? Or the rather startling surge of irritation he felt at the way the old lady made her sound like some sort of faithful cocker spaniel? Mrs. Vonnegut couldn't be describing the same stubborn, contentious little blonde he knew, could she?

Oblivious to his feelings, Mrs. Vonnegut chattered on. "She's generous, too. Why, last year she purchased new textbooks for her class with her own money. Of course, now that she's Mrs. Kincaid—"

"Ms. Cooper," Dare corrected. When Mrs. Vonnegut's eyebrows shot up, he shrugged and confided blandly, "We have a modern marriage. I keep my name—she keeps hers."

"Really?" After an initial look of surprise, she shrugged. "Well, be that as it may, young man, now that you're married, I would imagine she *will* have to be a little more careful about making such extravagant gestures." She cocked her head, rather like an oversize bird searching for a tasty crumb to gobble. "Unless, of course, you're independently wealthy? Just what is it you said you do for a living?"

He picked up a steel tape and began to double-check the dimensions of the door opening. "I didn't."

"Oh." She tittered, unabashed. "Well, that explains why I couldn't remember. When you get to be my age, sometimes you forget more things than you recall."

Dare glanced into the depths of her bright brown eyes and seriously doubted that. He'd bet his badge the old lady had a memory like a steel trap.

She smiled ingenuously. "So what *do* you do?"

"I've been working overseas."

"Doing what?" she persisted.

"Scheduling trips for a certain class of... businessmen."

"Hmmph." She considered for a moment. "You mean you're a travel agent."

"Actually, what I do is a little more specialized than that. I also see to their... security."

She tipped her head. "But if you've been out of the country, where did you meet Victoria?"

Cursing the warped sense of humor that had painted him into this particular corner, he reviewed the information he'd read in the schoolteacher's file. "We met on the cruise," he improvised, moving past Mrs. Vonnegut to reach the new solid-core door he'd had delivered.

Mrs. Vonnegut blinked. "What cruise?"

Puzzled, he watched her reaction carefully. "The one to the Bahamas that Victoria took earlier this summer."

The old lady looked startled. "This summer? Why, she never said a word about any cruise! She claimed she was going to a teaching seminar. A cruise and a husband... Ooh, that sly miss!" She made a thoughtful, tsking sound. "I wonder what else she hasn't told me?"

Dare's thinking was remarkably similar. *First the lingerie, now this. I wonder what else I don't know?*

The thought brought him up short. His expression turned speculative as his gaze zeroed in on the elderly neighbor lady. She wasn't the only person who could ask questions, he realized, hefting the new door and carrying it over to the opening. The thing was heavy; he felt the strain across his shoulders as he muscled it into place. "Yeah, Victoria is full of surprises. She looks so quiet, but every once in a while she does something you wouldn't expect."

Mrs. Vonnegut rose to the bait like a starving trout. "Isn't that the truth! Why, look at the way she's befriended that hooligan, Charles Wells. I do hope you're going to put a stop to that. If I've told Victoria once, I've told her a hundred times, no good can come of it, but she simply refuses to listen." Her mouth puckered with disapproval.

Dare used a nail to mark where the hinges needed to go, sorting through his memory for some clue as to Charles's identity. He carried the door over to a pair of old chairs he was using as sawhorses and laid it down before the information clicked in his mind, and he remembered that Charlie was the name of the boy Victoria tutored. He reached for a chisel and raised one eyebrow in polite inquiry. "Really?"

"Oh, yes!" She stepped spryly out of his way. "Absolutely. That boy has been nothing but trouble since he showed up. Not that his sister has been much of a role model, what with the way she took a job at the tavern right after she and William broke up. I can tell you, in my day, no decent woman, separated from her husband or not, would have considered such a thing."

Great. Ten seconds into the conversation and he didn't have the slightest idea who—or what—the old lady was talking about.

His frustration proved to be short-lived, however. Having found a willing audience, Mrs. Vonnegut was just getting warmed up. Seeing his confusion, she stepped closer and gave him a commiserating pat on the shoulder.

"How like Victoria not to explain. Why, sometimes, that girl is more closemouthed than a clam with lockjaw!" She gave a dramatic sigh. "Charles, you see, has only lived here for the past year. As I understand it, his parents divorced. I don't know what happened to the father, but when the boy's mother died, he came to live with his sister, Pamela, who is married to William Craig, the local plumber.

"I can tell you, Charles wasn't in town five minutes before he started causing problems. If he wasn't picking a fight, he was skipping school. And that—" she gave another dramatic sigh "—was only the start of it. Pretty soon a week didn't go by without some new story coming to light. Doreen Perry despaired of having him walk into her grocery store, claiming he was forever pilfering things. And Hiram Pratt swears he caught him out behind his house one night, swilling beer and smoking cigarettes!"

With true perversity, Dare found he liked the kid a little better with every word. Not that he approved of stealing. He didn't. But the rest of it hardly qualified the boy to be public enemy number one, and at least it was the sort of behavior Dare understood. He knew what it was like to be young and alone and angry about both—

What the hell was he thinking? This had nothing to do with him. He'd never even *met* this kid. This was a job, and that was all. He wasn't getting involved. Period.

Oblivious to his inner turmoil, Mrs. Vonnegut leaned even closer, her face set in lines of disapproval. "But you haven't heard the worst. Last winter, after everything William had done, taking Charles in like that, the boy snuck out to the Morrisey place where William was making an early-morning service call and *stole* his brother-in-law's service van! Then he crashed it into a tree! I ask you—how's *that* for gratitude?"

It wasn't much, obviously—which instantly piqued Dare's interest. "So why'd he do it?" he asked bluntly.

"What do you mean, why?" the old lady asked. "Because he's a juvenile delinquent, that's why!"

Instinct told Dare there was more to it, but he recognized a narrow mind-set when he heard one. "So what happened?"

"Why, the law finally caught up with him. He spent most of last spring at a juvenile facility near Bozeman." Mrs. Vonnegut sniffed. "It would've been longer than that if Victoria hadn't come forward and offered to be his sponsor."

"Hmm." Recalling the previous night's dinner conversation, Dare made a note to have a little talk with his counterfeit spouse about the difference between car theft and a "transportation" problem.

"What a debacle!" the old lady continued. "You can imagine how happy William was about that! My friend Maude Jenkins works as a clerk in the children's court, and she told me he nearly had apoplexy when Victoria interfered. Then, to top it off, he and Pamela separated, Pamela got that job as a bartender at the tavern and Charles was home before you could say 'boo!' Although—" her expres-

sion turned thoughtful "—I do have to admit that ever since
dear Victoria has taken an interest in him, the boy has been
on his best behavior...

"However," she sniffed again, "I might as well tell you,
I never did believe that snow-shoveling balderdash about
how they met."

"You didn't?" Dare laid the top hinge plate into the depression he'd hollowed out. It was a perfect fit. He was glad
something was going right since, once again, he didn't have
the slightest idea what Mrs. Vonnegut was talking about.
"Actually, I had a few questions about that myself."

"Yes, well, my friend Martha—she's Maude's younger
sister—is a substitute teacher at the school, and she told me
that—" She paused, an arrested expression stealing across
her face as a shrilling sound issued from her house. "Why,
I believe that's my phone. You'll have to excuse me." She set
off at a trot for the stairs. "I'd hate to miss something important."

"But what about—" Dare slammed his mouth shut.
Good God! There he went again. Less than twenty-four
hours in this hodunk little town and he was actually solic-
iting gossip from a woman he didn't know—and was fairly
certain he didn't like.

"Good luck with your home improvements, dear," Mrs.
Vonnegut called. "And be sure and tell Victoria I said
hello."

As quickly as that, she was gone, leaving him to his un-
settled thoughts—and with more questions than he had answers.

Her door was missing.

There was no denying the evidence of her eyes, Victoria
conceded, as she stood in the hallway and stared into the
kitchen. In its place, right smack where it used to hang, the
glass upper half allowing a cheerful stream of light into the

room, was a brand-new, solid wood door. Her old one had been . . . replaced.

She knew exactly who was to blame, too. Dare Kincaid was outside on the porch, clearly visible as he walked past the bank of windows with what looked like her screen door in his hands.

Quelling a rush of irritation—honestly, who did he think he was, changing her door without asking?—she took the opportunity to study him, telling herself that it came under the heading of *know thy enemy.*

He was dressed in old jeans, white leather sneakers and a garish Hawaiian shirt that was untucked and open down the front. His inky hair curled over his collar and waved behind his ears. The haze of dark stubble on his cheeks didn't detract at all from his good looks. On the contrary; it accentuated the clean line of his jaw and the chiseled strength of his face.

He walked in a moment later.

There was an awkward silence as they stared at each other. Dare was the first to recover. "'Morning." He strode across to the sink, turned on the water and began to wash his hands.

No more than three feet separated them. Victoria could smell the mingled scents of soap and sweat on his sun-warmed, work-warmed skin. Uncomfortable with so much raw masculinity, she cleared her throat and asked, with what she thought was considerable restraint, "What did you do to my door?"

"I replaced it."

"I can see that. But why?" She turned on the heat beneath the teapot.

He glanced around, searching for a dish towel. When he didn't see one immediately, he wiped his hands on the front of his shirt. How . . . civilized, Victoria thought, staunchly ignoring the way her heart skipped a beat as she got an eyeful of broad male chest.

Dare leaned back against the counter. "The thing was an intruder's dream. One quick rap on the glass and anyone could be inside in the blink of an eye."

"Still, you might have asked me if it was all right."

"Yeah. But I didn't, and it's too late now. Sorry." He sounded anything but.

The teapot whistled. She pulled it off the burner and took a pair of mugs down from the cupboard. "Would you like a cup of tea?"

He looked pained. "Nope. What I'd like is a cup of coffee. But unless you've got a secret stash, I'm damned if I can find any."

"I don't drink coffee. Sorry." To her chagrin, she didn't sound any more sincere than he had a moment earlier.

"I figured that."

She opened the refrigerator to retrieve the cream, only to frown when she didn't see it. That was odd. She was certain she'd purchased a new container yesterday when she'd gone to get the loaf of bread. "Have you seen a carton of half-and-half?" she asked Dare.

To her consternation, an almost furtive look came and went in his eyes before he said gruffly, "Nope."

She blinked. She'd seen that look before—from students who claimed the dog had eaten their homework or that their term paper had been stolen by aliens from another planet.

Except... why would he lie about such a thing? It made no sense. If he'd spilled it or—she quailed at the thought— drank it, or something, why wouldn't he just say so? He certainly hadn't been shy about saying anything else that came into his head.

She must be mistaken, she decided. She must have forgotten to get it, after all. Given the events of the past twenty-four hours, it wasn't surprising that her memory was a little muddled.

She forced her attention back to the subject they'd been discussing. "Do you really think a different door will keep someone from breaking in?'' she asked, swinging the fridge door shut.

"No, I don't." Was it her imagination, or was there a slight lessening of tension in him? "But it will slow them down, and that's the best we can hope for, given the situation."

"Oh." She considered his words. "Do deputy U.S. marshals normally masquerade as handymen?"

He walked across to the door and tested the new dead bolt. "Nope. But then, they don't usually live with their assignments, either. The s.o.p. for witnesses at risk is for them to retire to a motel or a safe house. Where—" his voice took on an ironic tone "—their security can be reasonably managed."

"S.o.p.?"

"Standard operating procedure."

"Oh." She frowned. "So why is my situation being handled differently?"

He shrugged. "Beats the hell out of me." Despite his words, there was a flash of something unsettling in his eyes.

She tried to decide what it was. Uneasiness? Evasiveness? Frustration? "You're not very happy about it, are you?"

His expression suddenly grew dispassionate. "I'm just here to do a job. My personal feelings don't enter into it." He snapped the bolt back and pulled the door open, clearly set on getting back to work. "Speaking of which, the dentist's office called."

"Oh, that's right." She watched, fascinated, as he rocked back and forth on the balls of his feet, the motion doing interesting things to the seat of his jeans. "I have an appointment on Friday," she added a little breathlessly.

"Not anymore you don't. I canceled it."

Her eyes shot to his. "What?"

"Yep. I brought in the mail, too. I've been through it and it looks okay—there wasn't much there but advertising stuff, anyway. Oh, and your next-door neighbor stopped by. She was asking questions about how we met. I told her it was on the cruise ship."

Victoria gave a little gasp. "You what? But that was my private business! Nobody knew—"

"They do now," he said blandly. And with that, he stepped outside and pulled the door shut behind him, effectively putting an end to the conversation.

Victoria kicked off her shoes and ran her toes through the plush throw rug that covered her bedroom floor. Grateful that the day was finally over, she pulled the bobby pins from her hair and set them in a pretty blue pottery bowl on her dresser. Sighing with pleasure, she shook out her hair and gave herself a brief scalp massage, glad of the room's serene atmosphere. Its white walls and high ceiling, bleached maple furniture and delicate pastel fabrics all blended together to make the room feel both lush and restful.

With a tired sigh, she padded over to the window seat. Outside, the late-summer twilight had begun to ripen to indigo, a perfect backdrop for a silver moon that was full and bright. From her vantage point, she could see most of the big backyard beneath its sheltering canopy of maple leaves. There was the rose garden against the far fence, the familiar sweep of lawn, the small gazebo where she'd gone as a teenager to gaze up at the summer stars and think—until Aunt Alice had put a stop to it, claiming Victoria needed to spend more time studying and less time daydreaming.

Shaking off the memory, Victoria sank onto the cushioned seat, drew up her feet and tried to relax. Almost immediately, however, her mind turned to Dare Kincaid, the badge-carrying puzzle the U.S. government had sent her. He was not a subject likely to relax any woman under eighty-five. She didn't understand him, she conceded, resting her chin on her bent knees. And every time she thought she had him pegged, he did or said something different from what she expected.

Take earlier tonight, for example. They'd dined on one of her specialties, burned meat loaf and mashed potatoes with lumps. Miserably aware of the meal's unappetizing quality, Victoria had been braced for him to make some snide comment or disparaging remark. In all fairness, she'd been tempted to say something herself.

Not Dare. Just like the previous night, he'd been chivalrously silent. Not only that, but he'd actually eaten the stuff, whittling off the charcoaled edges of the meat and navigating around the misshapen bumps in the potatoes as if it was standard fare.

She tried to tell herself that he was only attempting to make amends for his high-handed behavior earlier in the day. Lord knew, the arrogant way he'd made changes to the house and decisions about her life—without consulting her—had certainly been the actions of a stereotypical macho male.

But then again, there had been other contradictions to that behavior. For example, he didn't expect her to wait on him. Not only that, but he'd actually insisted on pitching in and doing his share of the household chores, whether it was making his own lunch or doing dishes. Yesterday, he'd even made up his own bed. Not that *she'd* wanted to do it. The last place she wanted to be was near Dare Kincaid's bed.

Still, she had to admit she was curious about him. Enough that she'd gone back through the newspaper to glean what personal information she could about him. There hadn't been much. He was thirty-five, single and had been a marshal for eight years. He'd spent several months in South America before he nabbed Mendelez.

Also, he'd apparently broken some sort of Marshals Service record with the bust, since it brought to three the number of fugitives on the Marshals Fifteen Most Wanted list he'd arrested in less than two years. According to the paper, it wasn't the first time he'd made the news. Three years earlier, he'd been commended for bravery after he and a fellow marshal were ambushed while transporting a protected witness to a major trial. The other marshal had been killed outright; Dare had been wounded, but had continued to protect the witness until other marshals could arrive.

Victoria shivered. Given the current circumstances, she supposed she should take comfort in her protector's proven bravery.

If only he weren't so good-looking. And if only there wasn't some perverse, unladylike part of her that refused to be intimidated by the reason for his presence—or put off by the less pleasing aspects of his personality. A part that breathed a little faster every time she got too close to his handsome face and to-die-for body.

As if to taunt her, the words he'd tossed at her—was it only yesterday?—whispered through her mind. *Say... I wanted you. Anytime. Anywhere. Anyplace. That I was after you to do all sorts of lewd, improper things....* Her cheeks grew pink as she found herself wondering *exactly* what sorts of things he'd meant...

She sighed. Ever since her birthday, nothing had gone quite right. There'd been the cruise, and then the incident regarding the judge, and now fate had sent her a perfectly gorgeous man with all the charm of a hedgehog. A man who regarded her with all the warmth most people reserved for an extensive IRS audit.

She tried to look on the bright side. The trial was scheduled for the first week in September, so it wasn't as if she had to put up with him forever. In less than two weeks, the entire experience would be behind her. Why, in a few years, she'd probably look back on the whole thing as a great adventure. She might even be able to find some humor in the incredible curve he'd thrown her by telling Doris Vonnegut they were married.

Be careful what you wish for... Aunt Alice must have said those words a thousand times while Victoria was growing up. But then, Aunt Alice had always been warning her about something.

Usually about herself and her untrustworthy heritage.

According to her aunt, Victoria's father had been an irresponsible daredevil who had lured Victoria's mother to her demise by refusing to quit the military and lead a settled, respectable life. While Victoria knew, with adult hindsight, that a man who reached the rank of lieutenant and flew million-dollar airplanes couldn't be a complete ne'er-do-well and that her mother's death had been nothing more than a tragic accident, her childhood had been colored by her aunt's warnings. She may not ever have forgotten her handsome, exciting, larger-than-life father, but she'd known early on that the price of Aunt Alice's approval was the suppression of any adventurous urges of her own.

Not that it had been so difficult to do. Despite Alice's somewhat narrow view of life, Victoria had always known her aunt genuinely loved her; she, in turn, had loved her aunt and wanted her approval. With a sensitivity beyond her years, Victoria had understood that part of the reason for her aunt's constant warnings was the elderly lady's fear of losing someone else she loved. Victoria had done her best to allay that fear. She'd been a good and devoted niece, and she'd worked hard to secure a respected place in the community—one that would make her aunt proud.

As a matter of fact, if you'd asked her a year ago, she would have said she was satisfied with her life. But gradually, in the past six months or so, she'd increasingly experienced moments when she felt restless and dissatisfied. As if life was passing her by. As if there was something waiting for her if she only had the courage to go looking for it.

Well, she had gone looking for it, she reminded herself—and look what a disaster *that* had turned into. It should serve as a reminder of how much she had to be thankful for.

She had a job she loved, the respect of her community and colleagues, food on the table and a substantial roof over her head. Granted, it might not be glamorous or exciting, but as Aunt Alice would have been quick to point out, it was safe and secure. Or it had been, until a certain deputy U.S. marshal had burst into her life....

The thought was so disturbing, it was almost a relief when a movement on the far side of the yard caught her attention. Or it would have been, if not for her sudden realization that what she was seeing was an intruder making his way toward her house. He stuck to the shadows next to the fence. There was no mistaking his air of furtiveness.

Victoria suddenly couldn't breathe. Terror splintered through her. She wondered wildly if the person who'd sent the threat was actually coming to get her. But then, as the figure paused and was caught in the light from Doris's stoop, she saw a glint of dark blond hair and realized it was Charlie.

Charlie—who'd had a tutoring session scheduled for earlier tonight that had completely slipped her mind, she abruptly realized.

Her fear subsided, replaced with uneasiness. It seemed pretty unlikely that he'd forgotten, too. But if he hadn't, if he'd deliberately stayed away, why? And why would he come by at this hour?

He wouldn't, she suddenly knew. Not unless something was wrong or he was in some sort of trouble.

She didn't stop to think. She shoved her hair back from her face, jumped off the window seat and dashed for the door, thankful she hadn't yet changed into her nightgown.

In the hall, she paused. The marshal's door was shut—and she wanted it to stay that way. Glad for the carpeted runner, she tiptoed down the hall, taking care not to make any noise. Once around the corner to the landing, she flew down the stairs and into the darkened kitchen.

There she slid to a halt, disconcerted to find that the spot on the porch where she expected to see Charlie was empty. Not only that, but the outside light was off...

What if she'd been mistaken? What if it hadn't been Charlie she'd seen, but someone else with blond hair? What if they'd tampered with the light, and were just waiting for her to step outside—

Stop being a ninny. Of course it was Charlie. He probably thought she was sleeping and wasn't certain if he should wake her, that was all. As for the light, the bulb was probably burned out.

She took a deep breath to rally her flagging courage, reminding herself as she did that she wasn't going to let fear run her life. Then she pulled open the door, pushed aside the screen and stuck her head outside.

The porch was a sea of shadows. Irritated to find her hands were shaking, she clenched them into fists. "Hello? Is anyone there?"

To her chagrin, her voice came out as nothing more than a tremulous whisper, creating barely a ripple in the utter stillness of the night.

Not surprisingly, nobody answered.

Victoria swallowed, took a deep breath and tried again. "Hello? If you're out here, please answer."

She jumped as a faint rustling came from her left, but it was only the breeze sighing through the trees. She pressed a hand to her chest, as if to physically subdue the erratic beat of her heart, which thundered so hard it hurt.

She decided to give it one last try. "Hel—"

"Would you shut up!" The disembodied whisper shot out of the darkness straight into her ear.

She gave a smothered shriek, only to have her heart bounce into her throat and wedge so tight she couldn't breathe, much less call out. She began to scramble backward, only to be stopped by a hand that materialized out of the murk. To her horror, it hooked in the front of her dress, causing several buttons to give way. She tried to bat it away, but instead it yanked her close, so that she found herself flush up against the steely heat of a man's solid, cotton-covered chest.

Victoria went wild. Clubbing her attacker in the midriff with her elbow, she felt a pang of satisfaction as she heard him go "Oomph." Her relief was short-lived, however, as a pair of arms like steel cables locked around her. A hand clamped over her mouth, and a deep male voice hissed, "Hold still, dammit!"

It was the marshal. Victoria nearly swooned with relief, only to have her heart leap again when she heard a scared but determined young voice call, "Hold on, Miss Cooper! I'll save you!" followed by the sound of running footsteps.

With a superhuman effort, Victoria shook off Dare's hold and tried to step around him. "Charlie, no!" she cried.

But she was too late. As she looked on with helpless horror, a figure came flying out of the darkness, hurled itself at Dare, and the two intertwined figures crashed against the screen and flew into her unlit kitchen with an ominous clatter.

Four

***

The witness protection detail from hell, Dare thought, as he and his attacker crashed into the kitchen table, slid across the top and smashed to the floor on the other side in a tangle of arms and legs.

But then, nothing about this assignment was going right. The house was a security nightmare, the schoolteacher refused to follow directions, and now, if he wasn't mistaken, the kid she tutored seemed to think *he* was the bad guy.

Damn. And all he'd wanted to do was replace the bulb in the porch light.

One thing was for sure, they weren't making kids the way they used to; while he was concentrating on defending himself and had yet to make an aggressive move, the boy wasn't pulling his punches. Even as Dare tried to roll out of reach, the kid hooked a leg around him and rammed his joined fists into Dare's solar plexus, in the exact spot where Victoria had elbowed him a few minutes earlier.

It hurt like the very devil, and suddenly he'd had enough. He rolled onto his back, blocked a punch aimed for his face and waited for the boy to take a second shot. When he did, Dare locked his fingers around the youngster's wrist, gave it a hard jerk and scooted out from underneath him, so that the boy slid onto the floor. He rolled to his feet, shoved a knee into the small of the boy's back, and pulled up and in on his wrist.

A fierce young voice rose out of the darkness. "Let go of me, you dirt bag!" Charlie cried, struggling futilely against Dare's hold. "I'm warning you—if you lay a hand on Miss Cooper, I'll pulverize you!"

Dare couldn't help it. His mouth twitched in amusement. The kid had moxie, even if he lacked common sense. "Listen, Rambo. You're not exactly in a position to threaten anybody. I'd advise you to shut up and hold still, unless you want to spend the next few months making friends with an orthopedic surgeon." To illustrate his point, he gave a warning tug on the boy's arm, prompting a grunt of frustrated fury and a spate of nasty expletives.

The next instant, Victoria turned on the switch above the stove, flooding the room with light. By the time Dare's eyes adjusted, she was standing over him, tugging on his arm. "Let go of him!" she ordered, as fierce as a little lioness defending her cub.

Dare caught her against him. "Calm down. *Sweetheart,*" he added meaningfully. He stared into the big blue eyes only inches from his own. "Before I do that, why don't you tell your young friend here to chill out? He seems to think I'm trying to hurt you."

Her eyes widened. "But how do you know—"

She looked different with her hair down. Soft. And...vulnerable. He wondered why he hadn't noticed before how pink and lush her mouth was. Then, as he felt his body stir, he wondered what the hell he was doing noticing it *now*.

He forced himself to focus on her question. "I know who he is because you nearly took out my eardrum screeching his name," he said dryly. "This *is* the kid you tutor, isn't it?" Abruptly aware of how good her slender curves felt against him, he let go of her with alacrity.

"Yes." Dragging her gaze away from his, she switched her attention to the boy on the ground. "That's him."

The boy squirmed. "You heard her! Let me up, you jerk!"

Dare wagged his head at the kid's nerve, but did as ordered.

Instantly, Charlie sprang to his feet and scrambled out of reach. Tall for his age, with thick honey blond hair and dark blue eyes beneath straight black eyebrows, he was a good-looking youngster—despite the fading evidence of a week-old black eye and a scabbed-over scrape on his chin. Apparently, Dare wasn't the only person he'd tangled with lately.

Charlie's gaze swung anxiously to Victoria. "Are you all right, Miss Cooper?" His tone seemed to suggest that somebody was going to be in big trouble if he didn't like her answer.

"I'm fine," Victoria assured him, her expression anxious as she scrutinized him in turn. "What about you?"

The boy rubbed his wrist and shrugged. "No big deal."

Dare didn't bother to hide his irritation. "Great. Now that we know everyone's terrific, would one of you like to tell me what's going on?" He turned to Victoria. "What are you doing up, running around, opening doors? And why is he here—" his gaze raked Charlie "—at this hour?"

Charlie and Victoria exchanged a look; the boy's expression closed like the door on a bank vault swinging shut.

Victoria stood there for a moment, staring at him, then turned to Dare. "If it's all right with you, I'd like to speak with Charlie alone for a moment first." She raised her eyes to him, beseeching him to grant her request. "Please?"

Dare tunneled a hand through his hair. He wanted in the worst way to refuse, but the truth was, he couldn't justify it, even to himself. As much as he'd like to give her a scathing lecture about the stupidity of her actions tonight—right before he locked her in the nearest closet and threw away the key—he was supposed to be acting like her husband, not her jailer.

"I'll tell you what," he said abruptly. "I'm going to go out and finish changing the bulb in the porch light. But when I come back in, I'm going to expect some answers." Not waiting for a response, he strode purposefully for the door.

He'd barely stepped onto the porch when Charlie spoke. "It's true, isn't it?"

Victoria's stomach knotted. "What's true?"

"That you and him—" the boy jerked his head toward the door "—are married."

"Good Lord." She dropped into the nearest chair, motioning Charlie to sit. "Where did you hear that?"

"At work. Mrs. Vonnegut came in, and I heard her talking. I didn't believe it," he admitted, his gaze never leaving her face as he sat down gingerly on the edge of the chair at right angles to hers. "Even when she went on about how you were keeping your own last name and everything, I figured she was just talking the way she always does, trying to make herself sound important. But she had it right, didn't she? I mean—that guy wouldn't be here, otherwise."

"Is that why you didn't come for your lesson?"

He shrugged. "I had to work. I was gonna call, but then I heard that and . . . Is it true?"

It was one thing to lie to the adults in the community, Victoria thought. Although she still didn't like it, tonight's excitement had served to graphically demonstrate the potential danger of the situation—and Dare's commitment to her safety. Not only that, but by revealing that Mrs. Vonnegut was telling anyone who'd listen everything she knew,

Charlie had just unwittingly made Dare's point about the need for secrecy.

Even so, everything in Victoria rebelled at having to lie to the boy. In her opinion, he'd already had too much experience with adults who conveniently adjusted their standards to suit their circumstances. Although they'd never spoken of it directly, she'd heard enough bits and pieces to form a fairly accurate picture of his life before he'd moved to Gage. His father had abandoned the family to take up with somebody new. His mother had turned to the bottle for comfort—until the bottle had turned on her. And when it came to his sister Pam, Victoria had often wondered who was raising whom.

One way or the other, all the significant adults in the boy's life, the people who he should have been able to trust, had played fast and loose with the truth. Victoria didn't want to join their ranks. Yet, if she told the truth, she didn't doubt he'd insist on trying to protect her—and she couldn't live with that, either.

She cleared her throat. "Charlie? Just listen, okay? The guy has a name. It's Dare Kincaid. I realize it must seem rather strange, him showing up this way. I have to admit I find it a little hard to explain, myself."

Charlie gave a gravelly chuckle, the sound completely devoid of any humor. "What's to explain? He's here, isn't he? I know what that means."

Victoria frowned. "I know what *I* think it means. But what do you think it means?"

He gave a self-deprecating shrug. "Simple. The way it is with my old man. And with Pam and Will when they were still getting along. Now that you've got someone else, you won't want me coming around anymore. I'd just be in the way."

Despite his offhand manner, the look in his eyes was suddenly old and tired.

Victoria couldn't bear it. "Nonsense," she said firmly. "As far as I'm concerned, nothing is going to change. Except that for as long as Dare is here, you'll have another adult friend besides me. Why, you never know... You might even like him if you give it a chance."

Are you out of your mind? shrilled the little voice in her head. The hunk may make beds and do dishes, but Mr. Rogers he's not.

Shh, she admonished herself. She'd find a way to convince Dare to go along. She'd take on the devil himself to spare Charlie's feelings.

Charlie, however, wasn't buying it. Pushing to his feet, he sent her a cynical look that made her feel as if she were the child and he the adult. "I wouldn't bet on it, Miss Cooper. Most guys don't want some kid hanging around when they're feeling ... romantic."

Victoria stood, as well. "Perhaps that's true, but my relationship with Dare is—different." Lord knew, that was the gospel truth. "I'm not saying you two are going to become best buddies, Charlie. Just ... give it a chance, okay?"

His answer was another shrug—this one noncommittal. "Yeah. Maybe. I don't know." He glanced at the clock. "I gotta go. Pam's off early tonight and her car is on the fritz. I don't want her walking home from the tavern alone."

"All right." Since there was nothing she could say to that, Victoria let him go.

She was still standing there thinking about it when Dare walked in. She watched warily as he closed the door.

"So." He gave her a quick, sideways glance. "You ready to talk?"

She sighed. "What happens if I say no?"

He shot the bolt and pushed in the lock. "Don't." He stepped to the nearest window and pulled down the shade. "Tell me instead that you explained things to the kid and got him straightened out."

Just the way he said it made her mad. As if Charlie were some sort of assignment he'd given her, instead of someone with feelings, someone who mattered. She drew herself up, determined that as far as this particular conversation went, she was not going to let him bully her. "Yes. I suppose I did."

"You told him we were married?"

"I didn't have to. He already knew. That's why he came by."

"Huh." His surprise was evident, but he recovered quickly, as if afraid if he gave her an opening, she'd point out that she'd tried to warn him. "So how'd he take it?"

"Not great. He seemed to think you wouldn't want him around."

"Yeah, well... he's right. Now that I've met him, I've decided this tutoring thing isn't a good idea."

Victoria felt as if an icy hand had closed around her heart. "But... why?"

He shrugged. "It's one thing for you to spend a few hours a week reciting multiplication tables with some Howdy-Dowdy type. It's something else to give the run of the house to a hothead with an overprotective streak. If a situation develops, I don't want some kid around who won't follow orders. Hell—I've already got you to contend with."

No wonder there was a price on his head. "Well, that's too bad, Marshal. Because I've already told Charlie that nothing is going to change." She took a deep breath. "Except that, perhaps, if he'll give you a chance, you two can be friends... or something."

He stopped dead, right in the middle of pulling down a second shade. He released it, impervious to the noise it made as it shot up, retracting wildly. He straightened to his full height and turned slowly to confront her. "You what?"

She sighed again. "You heard me."

"Yeah, you're right." His eyes glinted dangerously. "I did. Now *you* hear *me*. I'm not here to baby-sit some kid.

So you'll just have to *un*tell him. Explain that you made a mistake—or something."

His sarcastic tone grated on her nerves like a carrot peeler. She straightened, irritated by the way he had of looming over her, making her feel small and insignificant. "I don't think you understand. Charlie hasn't had an easy time of it. He's had some problems in his past and is just starting to get his life turned around. A rejection now could mean the difference between whether that happens or not."

Kincaid's expression grew shuttered. "Sorry, but that's not my concern. The kid'll survive. Kids are tough."

Victoria, who normally abhorred violence, wanted to kick him.

She settled for raising her chin. "You are, of course, welcome to your opinion."

He narrowed his eyes. "What the hell does that mean?"

"It means I refuse to tell Charlie he's not welcome here."

His expression darkened dangerously. "I thought we covered this earlier. You either do as I say or—"

"You'll lock me up?" Victoria considered it for all of half a second, then nodded. "Very well." She turned on her heel and headed for the stairs.

"Hey! Wait one damn minute!"

She could feel his eyes boring into her back like twin laser beams. "I think not."

"But we're not finished! We've still got some things to discuss—like what you thought you were doing ignoring rules two, five and six!"

Victoria stopped and looked at him over her shoulder. "If I'm going to jail, I don't need to remember your rules, Mr. Kincaid. I will, however, need some time to pack, but I'm sure I can be ready by first thing tomorrow morning."

And with that, she faced forward and sailed out of the room, chin up, shoulders back—and every fiber of her body quaking with dread at the reckless thing she'd just done.

* * *

Dare couldn't sleep. He gave up the pretense before dawn, got out of bed and pulled on a pair of jeans.

He padded into the kitchen, only to be instantly met with a soft but insistent mewling at the back door. He stood for a moment, racked by indecision. And then, cursing under his breath, he walked over, turned the dead bolt and opened the door, gazing through the screen into the grayness at the battered orange cat he'd encountered the previous morning.

He scowled at the beast. "Put a sock in it, would you?" He raked a hand through his disheveled hair. "What're you doing here, anyway? I thought we agreed you weren't coming back."

The creature, which was scrawny and potbellied, with a torn ear and a kink in its tail, stared owlishly back, and gave another plaintive meow.

He sighed. "Hungry, huh? Well, I can sympathize with that. Let me tell you, buddy, I haven't been eating too well myself lately." The cat meowed again; Dare told himself he was probably going to regret it, but let the feline in.

"Listen, Fuzz Face. I'm already in trouble for stealing the cream, you know. If the teacher finds out I raided her groceries for the likes of you, we're both gonna be in trouble." The cat twined around his ankles, making a grumbling noise low in its throat.

"Easy for you to say." He searched through the cupboards until he found a can of tuna. "After last night, she already thinks I'm lower than dirt." He opened the can and dumped the contents on a plate. "You can consider this a favor for both of us. At least she won't be able to make another tuna casserole." He carried the plate across the room and set it out on the porch.

The cat, its bent tail lashing in appreciation, pounced on the fish with greedy satisfaction. Dare gave the beast's bony little head a stroke with his thumb, then firmly shut and locked the door.

He made himself a cup of tea, telling himself it was better than nothing. Then he wandered out to the living room, where he sat down in the big wing chair situated in front of the window to watch the sun come up.

Despite his attempt at levity with the cat, he couldn't quit thinking about last night. The recollection of his own behavior rankled. He, who rarely lost his temper, who couldn't remember the last time he'd actually shouted at someone, had done both last night.

It was her. The teacher. There was just something about her that got to him. She was such a prim little thing, more restrained than an old maid's corset.

Except she hadn't seemed very proper last night. Not with her hair loose, tumbled around her shoulders like a cloud of spun gold. And not with her slim little feet bare and the first few buttons of her dress open, revealing the creamy swell of her delicate breasts.

Nor had there been anything shy and retiring about the stubborn, spirited way she'd stood her ground about the kid. Her announcement that she'd rather be locked up than risk hurting Charlie had struck at feelings buried deep inside Dare, chiseling away at the almost forgotten memories of another kid's desperate longing for an adult he could count on.

He took a sip from his mug and tried to shrug the memories off.

But for the first time in years, they refused to go away.

His had been a fairly typical family, one dad, one mom, one kid, until, like Charlie's, Dare's father had turned his back on his responsibilities and walked away. Dare had been ten, old enough to understand and be angry that something cataclysmic had happened, but too young to do anything to change it.

With no job skills to speak of, his mother had done the best she could by cleaning other people's homes. It had been barely enough to put food on the table, however; within six months, they'd been forced to leave the house in which Dare had grown up for a series of rented rooms.

Dare had done what he could to help. Big for his age, he'd worked whenever anyone would hire him, doing yard work, washing cars, running errands. But by the time he'd been old enough to get a job that would pay enough to really mean a difference, it had been too late. His mother, never robust physically or mentally, had started a slow slide into depression that saw her hospitalized on and off all through his high school years. Living by his wits, lying to everyone in authority, from his mother's doctors and social workers to the people at school, Dare had managed to keep a roof over their heads and himself out of foster care.

But it hadn't been easy. And the years with no one to trust, no one to rely on, no one to confide in, had left their mark, shaping the man he'd become. A loner. Independent, self-reliant, resourceful. And too damn smart, he told himself sternly, to let the memories of his own unhappy childhood influence him in this situation.

He'd learned the hard way that sentiment had no place on the job. He'd let friendship get in the way of judgment where Jimmy was concerned, and as a result Jimmy was dead. The man who'd taught him what being a marshal was all about, who'd come a hell of a lot closer to being a father to him than his own ever had...

He shook his head, his mouth twisting in self-disgust at the unruliness of his thoughts, and brought his mind back to the problem at hand: Victoria—and last night's noble gesture.

It had probably been just that, a gesture and nothing more, he told himself. Chances were, she hadn't meant a word that she'd said. Or she'd somehow figured out he was bluffing with his ''do what I say or else'' routine and had decided to call him on it. Either way, her announcement that she was willing to go to jail had probably been nothing more than a ruse intended to get her way and make him back off.

He turned the idea over in his mind, watching as the first fingers of dawn crept up over the far horizon. Flaxen streamers of light climbed into the sky, turning the pre-dawn grayness from charcoal to silver to mother-of-pearl. Lavender followed, shot through with streaks of flame and ribbons of magenta.

Yes. That was most likely it. One way or the other, her entire story would probably change with the rising of the sun.

With that realization, something inside him that had been coiled tight started to unwind. He drained the last of the now-lukewarm tea from his cup, stood and stretched, easing the tension across his shoulders.

He felt better now that he had things worked out, although he still didn't understand Ms. Cooper, much less trust her.

But then, he wasn't getting paid to.

Victoria found Dare in the kitchen later that morning. He was standing on a step stool next to the windows. He had the electric drill in his hand and was doing something to one of the sashes.

As usual, he looked lean, mean and dangerous. The quintessential male. She wondered how it was possible to find someone you didn't like wildly attractive. She wondered why she cared. And she wondered what he was doing to the window, and why he was bothering, given the way they'd parted last night.

She supposed she might as well find out.

"Good morning," she said when the whir of the motor faded away. She took a deep breath to calm her roiling stomach and walked farther into the room.

It was a moment before he looked at her. His smoky gaze went from her face to the suitcase in her hand before he turned his attention back to the window sash. His expression was infuriatingly blank. "You slept late."

She'd hardly slept at all. She'd been up most of the night, asking herself what she thought she was doing. When she'd decided months ago that she'd like a little adventure in her life, going to jail wasn't quite what she'd had in mind. Yet every time she remembered that bleak look in Charlie's eyes before he'd walked out the door last night, she realized she had no choice. If she was going to be a prisoner, she was darned if it was going to be in her own home, with Dare Kincaid as her jailer.

Still, she was determined to be civil—even if it took a mammoth effort. Aunt Alice had often stated that the true test of a lady was the way she comported herself during the worst of times, not the best.

This certainly qualified as far as she was concerned. "What are you doing?"

"I must've skipped this window yesterday. I'm getting ready to install a bolt."

"Why?"

He made a quick, impatient sound. "Same theory as the door. A lock may not stop someone, but it'll slow 'em down—"

"No." She stood a little straighter. "I mean, why are you doing this . . . now? When I'm ready to go?"

He brushed a film of sawdust off the sash, sending dust motes flying through the sunlight that poured through the window like liquid gold. "Go where?"

She was rapidly running out of patience. "To jail."

"Oh, that." He stepped down and laid the drill on the floor, his time-whitened jeans seriously strained by the expansion of muscle in his hips and thighs. He walked over to the counter, picked up a brass fitting and some screws and tossed the whole works into his shirt pocket. "Yeah, well, forget it. I changed my mind."

He'd changed his mind? She couldn't have heard him right. She'd been up all night, tossing and turning, worried sick, envisioning handcuffs and strip searches and prison guards who were a cross between Hulk Hogan and Cruella DeVille—and he'd changed his mind?

She set her suitcase down and pushed it carefully under the table, afraid if she didn't, she'd throw it at him. She managed to keep her voice level but it took a monumental effort. She had to repeat Aunt Alice's maxim about the true test of a lady twice. "Why?"

He turned, the motion causing his unbuttoned shirt to gape open, giving her a clear view of his sculpted chest.

Victoria refused to be distracted. She didn't care if he stripped off the rest of his clothes and danced the hokey-pokey in his underwear. She wanted an answer. She wanted one *now*.

What she got was a nonchalant shrug of his big broad shoulders. "I'm not in the mood."

She was so incredulous, she forgot to be angry. "You're not in the *mood?*"

He sighed, a long-suffering sound, and leaned back against the counter. He folded his arms across his chest. "Hey, look," he said reasonably, "I never said a word about any of this last night. You brought it up. Remember? You jumped to a conclusion about what I was going to say and then you just...went with it, storming out before I could set you straight."

She was so stunned by the sudden shift in his manner that she actually thought about what he was saying. Technically, he was right, she realized. But she also knew darn well the only reason he hadn't said the actual words himself was because she'd beat him to it. From the guarded, almost defensive look on his face, she could see he knew it, too.

Yet, for whatever reason, he was backing down. She couldn't imagine why, but at the moment she didn't care. All that mattered was that he had. The knowledge swept through her on a tidal wave of relief that sent her sliding onto the nearest chair. "Thank goodness." She glanced fixedly down, struggling for composure. When she finally gained control of her emotions, she looked up to find he was staring straight at her.

His gray eyes were narrowed, a look of uneasiness making them darker than normal. "You were really worried, huh?"

She thought about all the terrible things she'd imagined and shivered. "Yes."

"But you were going to go through with it."

"Yes."

"Why?"

She hesitated, convinced that he'd make fun of her if she told the truth but unable to think of a good lie. "Charlie Wells is my friend," she said finally. "I care about him."

His gaze touched her suitcase before coming back to her face. "And for that, you'd risk jail?" He was silent a moment before he slowly shook his head. "I don't get you."

This from a man with more ups and downs than a bungee jump. She didn't get him, either, but she wasn't about to say so. Not until she knew precisely where they stood. "I'm sorry. I'm not trying to be difficult." She sent him a tentative smile. "Maybe—if we both made an effort—do you think we could try to get along?"

A quicksilver flash of surprise lit his eyes. He picked up a screwdriver and pushed away from the counter, moving back to the ladder. "Sure."

"What about Charlie?"

"What about him?"

"Is it okay for him to come around?"

Planting one foot on the bottom rung of the ladder, he swiveled to look at her. "You don't let up, do you... Victoria?"

It was the first time he'd used her name. It sounded different coming from him. Disturbing, somehow. "I don't want any more misunderstandings."

He turned back, fished the window lock from his pocket and positioned it over the starter holes he'd drilled. "Is that what you think last night was?" he asked, as he set a screw in place. "A misunderstanding?"

She watched the muscle in his arm bulge as he deftly twisted the screwdriver. Finished quickly with the first screw, he set a second one in place, holding it between his thumb and forefinger to get it started. "No," she said quietly. "It was me being foolish and careless. What I did, barging downstairs and opening the door that way, was stupid. I'm sorry."

He was so surprised, he jerked his head around—and promptly sliced open his palm when the screwdriver slipped. "Sonofa—" The screwdriver clattered to the floor. He clamped his teeth together and stepped back off the stool, cradling his wounded hand in his uninjured one.

"Oh, dear!" Victoria leaped to her feet and was at his side without quite knowing how she got there. "I'm sorry. I didn't mean to distract you." She wrapped a hand around his elbow and tugged him toward the sink.

"Relax. It's no big deal," he protested, despite the blood steadily welling up.

She flipped on the cold water, took him by the wrist and pushed his hand under the stream of water. "Leave it there," she said, when he tried to pull back. "There may have been metal shavings on the screwdriver." She let go of him to yank open a drawer and retrieve a pair of clean kitchen towels.

When she was satisfied the cut had been sufficiently flushed, she turned off the tap, dried his hand with one towel, then folded the other and used it to dab gingerly at the wound. She frowned at the way the blood continued to ooze out. "This may need stitches," she told him, reaching into the cupboard for the emergency medical kit.

He pressed down on the cloth and shook his head. "Forget it."

"But the doctor should probably—"

"It's just a scratch," he said stubbornly.

She glanced over. His mouth was set in an intractable line. "All right." She opened up the kit, uncapped a bottle of hydrogen peroxide and dampened a piece of sterile gauze. She slid one hand under his to steady it, took away the towel and pressed the disinfectant to the wound. It had to sting, but he didn't make a sound. After a few seconds, the bleeding slowed.

Catching her lower lip between her teeth in concentration, Victoria used some small bandages to butterfly the edges of the cut together, then put a piece of sterile gauze over them, holding it in place with some strips of cloth adhesive tape. "You're going to need to keep that clean and dry."

"Whatever you say."

She looked up, suddenly aware that they were standing so close she could see little flecks of silver in the darker gray of his irises. His hand was still nestled in her palm; she could feel its heat against her cooler skin.

He stared down at her. His expression was impossible to read. "Are you always this bossy?"

His face was only a hand's width away. He had a tiny, triangular scar edging his bottom lip. Her own mouth suddenly felt cotton dry. She swallowed. "No—yes... sometimes, I guess. It's because I'm accustomed to being in charge in the classroom, I imagine."

His gaze drifted a fraction lower, touched her trembling mouth. Something dark and hot flared in his eyes, setting off an answering ripple of heat inside her. He lifted his gaze to her. "Thanks for the first aid, anyway." His voice was low and hushed in the sudden quiet.

He was going to kiss her. She could see it in his face, in the slightly predatory cast that had come over his features. The knowledge sizzled along her veins, exploded in her brain.

She wanted to kiss him, too, she realized. It was sheer madness. She didn't know him, would have sworn ten minutes ago that she didn't like him, but she still wanted to kiss him. She could imagine the satiny firmness of his mouth against her lips, the slick slide of his tongue nudging her own...

Suddenly shy, she dropped her gaze, only to find herself staring at his bare stomach. She'd never been so close to a man's naked stomach before; his was washboard flat and bisected by a dark swirl of hair that ran over the shadowed depression of his navel and under the low-riding snap of his jeans.

She couldn't drag her eyes away. A haze of heat rose from deep inside her. She wondered how it would feel to touch him. To slide her hands inside his shirt and stroke her palms over his taut golden skin. To discover for herself if he felt the way he looked, like sun-warmed satin. To trail her fingertips down the silky line on his belly and—

Not daring to think any further, she shut her eyes and raised her face to his, her lips parted in anticipation of his kiss.

She waited, counting the beat of her pounding heart. One... two... three...

Nothing happened. She opened her eyes. Dare was inches away, staring intently at her, his eyes riveted to her mouth, the skin across his cheekbones oddly taut. She could feel the heat rush into her face as it dawned on her that he was just standing there, not making a move to do... anything.

Their eyes met; his were impenetrable, the opaque gray of a concrete wall. He straightened abruptly, his expression shuttered. "I'd better get back to work." Stepping around her, he moved as if he couldn't get away fast enough.

Victoria had never been so humiliated. She stood, facing the sink, her shoulders bowed, thankful her back was to him. What on earth had she been thinking? She'd practically thrown herself at him. Had the combination of a sleepless night and a rush of adrenaline at the sight of a little blood unhinged her completely? Or was this simply another example of the Cooper tendency toward impetuousness that Aunt Alice had warned her about?

The thought was like a splash of cold water. Obviously, she couldn't trust herself where he was concerned. There was something about him, hormones or pheromones or just plain old be-still-my-heart-moans—that acted on her like a sexual call of the wild. Fortunately for her and her continuing virtue, it was clearly one-sided. But while he'd been a gentleman once and saved her—saved them both—from making a terrible mistake, it was up to her to make sure that it didn't happen again.

She took a deep breath, then straightened her shoulders. She could do that, she told herself. She would just have to match his composure, pretend that she hadn't just embarrassed them both, and give him a wide berth in the future.

But first, the issue of Charlie had to be resolved.

She began to pile things in the medicine kit, determined to act as if nothing was wrong and to prove she could behave like a mature, reasonable adult. "I really am sorry about last night," she said, finding safety behind a screen of words. "About breaking your rules. I saw Charlie from my window. Normally, he doesn't come by so late, so I was afraid something was wrong."

She forced herself to turn, only to have her mouth go dry as he stooped to pick up the screwdriver and she found herself staring right at the very tight, very male contours of what she'd once overheard one of her students refer to as a tush. She tried to smile, but her face felt stiff. "I got worried and didn't think."

"Forget it." He straightened and walked over to the ladder. "And before you ask again, yeah, the kid can come for his lessons. For now, at least."

She blinked, surprised at how easy that had been. "Thank you."

"Don't let it go to your head," he said brusquely. "I'm going to expect you to toe the line on everything else." He climbed back up on the first rung of the step stool.

Victoria nodded. "You have my word," she said earnestly. "I won't give you one more second of worry."

He looked at her then, and something she couldn't define came and went in his eyes. It made her feel strange, which only reinforced her conviction that it would be best if she avoided him in the future. She raised her chin, gathering her resolve. After all, it was only ten days until she was due to testify.

How hard could it be?

Five

___

"Cool bike."

Dare looked up from where he was hunkered down beside the Harley. Charlie Wells was some half-dozen feet away, one shoulder propped against the side of the detached garage that doubled as Victoria's toolshed.

Dare acknowledged him with a slight nod. "Yeah, it is." He positioned a plastic bucket, then used a wrench to loosen the plug on the cycle's oil pan.

"You're changing the oil, huh?" The boy's pose was studiously casual, his thumbs caught in the belt loops of his jeans, one foot crossed in front of the other. His gaze was watchful.

"That's right." Out of the corner of his eye, Dare saw Victoria glance up. She was sitting about twenty-five feet away at a round metal table in the gazebo. Hard at work on her lesson plans, she was surrounded by books and papers. The warm afternoon breeze ruffled her pale hair.

She'd been working steadily ever since the morning he'd come within a hairbreadth of kissing her. Quiet and cooperative, she'd done every single thing he asked. She'd written out her schedule. She'd cooked—atrociously but without complaint. She'd dutifully made arrangements for someone to cover for her at the town health clinic. She hadn't said a word when he told some lady on the phone he didn't give a flying fig that Miss Cooper had collected money for the Adopt A Wild Horse fund for the past eight years, she wasn't doing it this year.

She hadn't even complained when she'd gone in earlier to make lunch, discovered the leftover chicken from last night's dinner was gone, and he'd told her he'd thrown it out rather than admit having fed it to a certain furry friend of his.

Just as she'd promised, she hadn't disagreed with him or done one contradictory thing in two days.

It was driving him stark, staring crazy.

He didn't understand her. You could've knocked him over with a feather when she'd shown up hauling her suitcase the other morning. After all his reasoning to the contrary, the evidence that she'd meant exactly what she said had thrown him off balance. As had her concern when he'd cut his hand. He'd been taking care of himself for so long that her desire to minister to him and her genuine distress had caught him by surprise, and he hadn't known how to respond.

It was the only explanation he had for how close he'd come to kissing her. The last thing he'd expected when she started fussing over him was that he'd feel that sudden slash of desire. But dammit, she'd been so transparent about what she wanted, so trusting the way she'd lifted her face to his and offered him her lips. Something about it had set off a fire in his blood he was still trying to stamp out.

He'd wanted to slide his mouth along hers, taste the pale pink promise of her lips, bury his face against the pulse beating wildly in her throat. He'd wanted to open the buttons of her dress, part the fabric and stroke her breasts. He'd wanted to lift her onto the counter, toss her skirt out of his way and see her eyes widen as he ran his hands up the inside of her thighs...

Which would've been a big-time stupid thing to do. He was here to protect her, not take her to bed, no matter how tempting. Even if she wasn't in imminent danger—and, as the days passed without so much as a hint of another threat, that seemed more and more likely—there were other things he had to consider. Primary among them was that she was a nice, respectable woman, leading a nice, respectable life. Even if he was willing to set aside his own rule about not mixing business with his personal life—which he was not, he reminded himself sternly—she was not the woman to do it with.

So what was his problem? Why did he feel so edgy and out of sorts? Why did her polite withdrawal gall him so much? He couldn't believe he really missed sparring with her, seeing how fast he could make her blush or get a rise out of her. But if not, then what? Could it be something as simple as frustrated lust?

He rejected the idea out of hand. He wasn't a man who let his libido dictate to him. Maybe, he thought slowly, he was feeling guilty. After all, she was being a damn good sport, all things considered. Once over the initial shock of having him call the shots in her life, she'd really made an effort to cooperate. She hadn't pouted or moped or sulked the way some women would to get their own way. She hadn't cried or complained. Even the past two days, when he suspected she was smarting from that aborted kiss, she'd made an effort to be pleasant.

Distant, but pleasant.

He shifted uncomfortably as he contrasted her behavior with his own. It was possible, he conceded, that he'd been a little insensitive when he'd settled on a cover story without consulting her. And he supposed the way he'd replaced the back door, and generally taken on securing the house without discussing it with her, might be construed as slightly arrogant—even though it was for a good cause. And he had been a trifle abrupt on a few occasions. Maybe it was time he cut her some slack. Chances were, he'd feel better if he did. After all, it wasn't her fault he'd been assigned to protect her, and they were in this together . . .

A shadow sliced across his vision as Charlie came closer. "You have to change the oil on a Harley very often?"

Dare shrugged. "Every fifteen hundred to two thousand miles. I don't know exactly. This isn't my bike."

"Really?" The boy ambled over to get a better look at the instrument panel. "Whose is it?"

"Friend of mine let me borrow it."

"Hmm. Some friend."

"Yeah." Dare watched the dirty oil pour into the bucket. "You like motorcycles?"

"They're okay."

"Ever ride one?"

Charlie's chin rose slightly. "Sure. Not a Harley, but my dad had a dirt bike. He used to let me ride it." He ran his finger over the padded leather seat. "Of course, it's been a while. I was just a kid."

It was a hell of a thing for a fourteen-year-old to say. Yet Dare understood it. Too well. Disturbed by the realization, and by the odd pang he felt as he glanced up at Charlie's dispassionate face, he changed the subject.

"So what're you doing here today?" The question wasn't idle; the kid had come by yesterday to make up the tutoring session he'd missed Thursday. As far as Dare knew, he hadn't been due back until next week. Yet here he was.

As if he could read Dare's mind, the youngster's expression turned defensive. "I came to mow the lawn."

If there was one thing Dare hated more than feeling maudlin, it was the idea that some chip-on-the-shoulder kid thought *he* was predictable. "You always mow on Sundays?"

Charlie gave him a long look, as if searching for some trap. "No," he said finally.

Dare waited a few seconds. When it became clear that was all the kid intended to say, he almost smiled. *He* knew the drill. *Volunteer nothing.* "So when do you?"

The boy relaxed at his mild tone. "Saturdays. Only, one of the other guys got sick so I had to work yesterday. Miss Cooper said I could just forget about it, but I want to get it done. The mower clogs if the grass gets too long."

"You have a job?" In a town this size, jobs for teens must be few and far between, making the competition for them keen. Given the kid's purported history, Dare found it interesting anyone would employ him.

Charlie fidgeted. "I work part-time as a box boy at the grocery store."

"Which one?"

"The only one. The Gage Market."

Dare's curiosity sharpened as he recalled what Mrs. Vonnegut had said about Charlie stealing. Unless . . . "Really? Must be nice. But aren't you young to have so much responsibility?"

The kid stiffened, then raised his chin and looked Dare straight in the eye. "Miss Cooper got me the job. I had to work for free the first month. Restitution, Miss Cooper called it—to pay back Mrs. Perry for a bunch of stuff I ripped off." Jaw bunched, he waited for Dare's reaction, braced on the balls of his feet like a fighter.

Again, Dare recognized the ploy. God knew, he'd used it often enough when he was a boy, tossing his "badness" in other people's faces, attempting to drive them off before they could get too close to him. "Yeah, well . . . good for you," he said, careful to maintain a neutral expression. "It takes a lot of backbone to face up to your mistakes."

Charlie gave a start of surprise, then tried to appear as if Dare's opinion didn't matter one way or the other. He shrugged. "I guess," he said, with a dismissive toss of his head. "I'd better get started." He set off for the garage.

Dare watched him go, disturbed by the strong sense of identification he felt. Shaking his head at such foolishness, he dismissed it as nothing more than empathy for a kid who'd had a bad time, and turned his attention back to the bike. He finished changing the oil, then began to tinker with the cycle's engine, trying to decide if it was improperly set timing or a bad spark plug that was causing it to miss and sputter occasionally.

He'd always enjoyed working with his hands, but today there was something especially soothing about it. He suspected it had to do with the day and the setting. It was one of those perfect summer afternoons, the sky as blue as a jay's wing, the air fragrant from the roses that dominated the garden. The fenced-in backyard was very private, a feeling that was reinforced by the leafy canopy of trees that sighed and shifted overhead. There was a sense of being cut off from the world, and between it, the drone of the lawn mower and the warmth of the sunshine—and five days without caffeine—he could feel himself relax.

He gave the dusty bike a once-over, thinking it was definitely in need of a wash. Deciding he might as well have a go at it, he checked the garage for supplies but didn't find what he needed, so he set off for the gazebo to ask Victoria where he could find them.

She looked up at his approach, a reserved, watchful expression in her eyes despite her pleasant expression.

"You have a bucket and some rags I can use to wash my bike?" he asked.

"Sure." She closed a loose-leaf notebook and came to her feet, smoothing the skirt of her shapeless lavender print dress against the breeze. As she came down the trio of steps, a playful gust lifted her hem, exposing shapely calves and delicate knees. "I'll get them. I keep that sort of thing in the pantry."

He knew it was perverse, but now that he'd decided to be nicer, her wariness rankled. Almost as much as the realization that there was a part of him itching to know what was hidden under that concealing dress. "You don't have to wait on me." He fell into step with her as she walked unhurriedly toward the house.

"I know, but I was about to head in, anyway. I thought I'd make some ice tea. I'm thirsty and I'm sure Charlie will want something to drink by the time he gets done. It's hot."

He couldn't think of a thing to say to that, so he shut up and dropped back half a stride to follow her up the stairs. He was right behind her when she reached the top and the loud popping noise erupted from the yard.

A second later, one of the kitchen windows shattered.

Dare didn't think. He reacted, throwing himself on top of Victoria, tossing her to the ground. "Stay down!" he ordered, rolling her behind the solid cover of one of the porch supports. With his forearm braced across her shoulders to keep her flat, he drew the gun hidden beneath the loose drape of his shirt at the back of his waistband.

There was no more gunfire.

Scanning the yard and the surrounding area for movement or any other sign of a concealed shooter, he realized there'd never been any in the first place.

There was only Charlie, standing frozen at the base of the stairs, his hands up in the classic stance of surrender, his face a study in horror. "Don't shoot!" he cried, his eyes riveted on the gun. "I didn't mean to break the window—honest! The mower threw a rock and— Oh, my God! Is Miss Cooper all right?"

Dare cursed, low and creatively, as the adrenaline rushing through him subsided a notch. No wonder Arizzo had banished him to the boonies. He was in sorry shape when he couldn't tell a rock tossed by a lawn mower from a gunshot.

He set the safety on the gun, shoved it under his shirt and rose to his feet. "Relax, kid. She's fine."

What the hell else could go wrong?

"I don't understand." Blue eyes narrowed with suspicion, Charlie stared stonily at Dare. With the resiliency of youth, once he'd found out Victoria was all right, the youngster had recovered quickly from his fright—and promptly launched into his personal version of the Spanish Inquisition. "I know I heard Mrs. Vonnegut tell Mrs. Perry you're a travel agent."

Seated opposite the boy at the kitchen table, Dare struggled with a curious mixture of amusement and exasperation. What was it with this town, anyway? Wasn't it indignity enough he was being grilled by a kid too young to drive? Was there some kind of 1-800 number you could call for the latest gossip, too?

Yet, he had to admit he admired the kid for his determination to look out for Victoria. As long as it didn't get out of hand. "Look, she may have said that. But like I've already told you, she only got it half right. What I said was, I arrange security for people making international trips."

The boy didn't look convinced. "You're not on a trip now," he countered with irrefutable logic. "So why are you carrying a gun?"

Dare made no effort to contain his sigh. "I told you that, too. It's a habit. Like brushing your teeth."

"But according to what you just said, you *arrange* security—you don't provide it." Charlie crossed his arms stubbornly across his chest. "If that's true, why do you need a gun? And if it isn't, and you're really a bodyguard, or something, how come you don't have a concealed weapons permit?"

Victoria set down a tray holding a pitcher of tea and three glasses. "Charlie," she said quietly. "Please—just drop it. Dare already explained how his wallet was stolen. I don't understand why you're acting this way."

The boy's face softened for an instant as he looked over at her. He shook his head. "You're too trusting, Miss Cooper. I mean, how much do you really know about this guy?" He gestured in Dare's direction. "You take a trip and then he shows up one day and all of a sudden you're married. How do you know he's not a con artist, or something?"

"Oh, for heaven's sake." Victoria made an exasperated sound as she filled a pair of glasses and handed one to him and one to Dare. "Do you really think I'm that gullible?"

To Dare's secret amusement, Charlie suddenly found it hard to look her in the eye. "It happens all the time," he said, backpedaling in an attempt to spare her feelings. "It doesn't have anything to do with how smart you are. Some sweet talker shows up and sweeps you off your feet… Look at Pam. She bought that whole line Will was feeding her and all the time he was—" A look of distaste swept across his face. "Well, you know." He slouched lower in his chair. "How do you know this guy's not going to do the same? Or worse?" he added darkly, with a menacing glare for Dare.

"Because." Victoria slid onto the chair beside him, her tone patient and reasonable. "Out there on the porch, when he thought there was a problem, his first thought was for my safety."

Charlie's gaze shot from Dare to her. There was a moment of charged silence as the truth of her statement sank in, and then he made a noise like the air escaping a balloon. "Oh…" A tide of red crept up his neck; even his voice sounded deflated. "You're right. I didn't think of that."

Victoria reached over and gave his arm a quick squeeze. "It's okay." She picked up the pitcher and poured herself a glass of the caramel-colored tea, her voice pitched so low, it could barely be heard over the clink of the ice cubes. "What's important is you cared."

The red tide of embarrassment in the teenager's face became a flood. Yet, as Dare had observed during his first encounter with the boy, Charlie Wells had spunk. He took a deep breath and, with the air of a condemned man about to confront a firing squad, turned to Dare. "I'm sorry. I was...out of line."

It was the perfect opportunity. All Dare had to do was pretend to be offended and tell the kid it would be best if he didn't come around for a while. Given the circumstances, it would be an understandable reaction, if not a very commendable one. Even if Victoria objected, the boy's own chagrin would probably be enough to keep him away. It would make security for the next eight days a hell of a lot less complicated.

Yet, as Dare looked into Charlie's eyes, he saw that was exactly what the kid expected—and suddenly he knew he wasn't going to do it. There was no use trying to kid himself, either. His decision had nothing to do with not wanting to be thought predictable—and everything to do with the unexpected sense of connection he felt with the prickly youngster.

"Forget it," he said brusquely. Charlie's eyes widened in amazement, and the next thing Dare knew, he was digging in his pocket for the key to the Harley. "Can you do me a favor?"

"I guess so," Charlie said uncertainly.

"Put the bike in the garage for me, okay? I'll wash it another day." He tossed the boy the key.

Charlie snatched it out of midair. "You mean it?"

"Yeah." Dare nodded. "Go on, get out of here."

"Cool." With an eagerness that was almost painful to see, Charlie bounded for the door without another word.

The screen door slapped shut. The room was silent except for the tick of the clock and the soft hum of the refrigerator. Victoria looked over at Dare. "Thank you," she said quietly. "That was nice."

He shrugged. "No big deal."

"It was to Charlie," she said, her sense of fair play dictating she give him credit where it was due. Having done that, there was no reason to linger, however. Particularly when it was probably wise to end the conversation *before* she noticed how attractive he looked with his ebony hair tumbled over his forehead.

She pushed back her chair and came to her feet. "Well," she said briskly. "I really should get back to work—"

He leaned forward and laid a detaining hand on her arm. "Hold on a minute."

His touch went through her like an electric shock. Self-preservation urged her to bolt for the door; pride held her in place as she took in his polite expression and realized the only person she'd be running from was herself. *He* certainly wasn't affected.

She sank back down, stung by the realization that two days of distance hadn't done a thing to temper her physical reaction to him. "What?"

He drew a line with his thumb through the condensation beading his glass. "I didn't hurt you out there, did I?"

"I'm fine." And eternally grateful he didn't appear to notice the little tremor that went through her as she drew back and his fingers slid from her elbow to her wrist and across the back of her hand before he released her.

"Good. Most people find they're pretty played out after a scare like that. It has to do with the sudden flood of adrenaline through your bloodstream. When it's over, you feel lower than a doormat."

She leaped at the lifeline he'd unwittingly thrown her. "You're right." She again started to rise to her feet. "I do feel tired all of a sudden. Maybe I should go upstairs and lie down."

His hand stilled on his glass and he looked up, pinning her in place. He gave her a long, considering look. "You aren't afraid of me, are you, Teach?"

Her common sense shouted, "Yes." It was drowned out, however, by the unmanageable little voice in her head, which got to her vocal cords first and said, with more audacity than sense, "Don't be ridiculous."

"Good." He sat back, stretched out his legs and crossed his arms over his chest. "So why don't you quit bobbing up and down like a pogo stick and tell me about the kid."

She perched on the edge of the chair, regarding him warily. "What do you want to know?"

"How'd you meet him, anyway? Was he one of your students last year?" His voice was low, perfectly matched to the mix of sunlight and shadow dappling the homey room.

It had the intended effect. She relaxed slightly. "No. He'll be in my class this year. As for how we met..." She hesitated. She'd never told anybody the true story. Nor did she want to prejudice Dare against Charlie just when it looked as if he'd decided to given the boy a chance.

On the other hand, she doubted anything could shock him. And based on her experience with him the past week, she knew he'd pretty much do and think whatever he wanted, regardless of what she said. And for all his toughness, the way he'd dealt with Charlie today had shown an unexpected sensitivity...

"So?"

He looked at her expectantly and she decided to take a chance. "It was last year, a few weeks after Christmas. I walked into my classroom with a colleague at lunchtime and there he was, going through my purse."

Dare's eyebrow rose. It was obviously not what he'd expected. "He was stealing from you?"

She nodded. "He had a twenty-dollar bill in his hand."

He thought about it for a moment. "Obviously, you didn't turn him in. How come?"

"I'm not sure I can explain. I knew who he was, of course. His reputation had...preceded him." She shook her head, her expression thoughtful. "For all his defiance, he seemed so defeated. He looked over at me and said, 'Hey, Miss Cooper,'" she mimicked the boy's contralto perfectly, right down to his tough-guy tone, "'Lucky you. You caught me.'"

The moment was seared on her memory. Guilt, fear and shame had kaleidoscoped across Charlie's face before he hid it behind a wall of contrived indifference.

"And?"

Victoria sighed and shook her head. "I don't know... Something in me rebelled. He was too young for such cynicism, too smart to have already given up. I wanted to prove to him that life could still hold a few surprises. So I said, 'Oh, good. You found the money.' And then I turned to my friend and said, 'Isn't that nice, Martha? Charlie's going to shovel my walks this month.'"

"You let him keep the money?"

"I gave him an opportunity to earn it," she corrected. "I walked over and retrieved my purse, told him I'd expect him after school and that he shouldn't be late. You should've seen his face."

"I can imagine," Dare said dryly. "How'd you know he'd show up?"

"Oh, I didn't."

"Then why bother?"

She shrugged. "If he didn't come, I was only out twenty dollars. But if he did... Well, I thought perhaps we might both make a friend."

Dare just looked at her. "You took a hell of a chance. What if he'd shown up, knocked you on the head and robbed you blind?"

"Oh, good grief. Give me some credit, please. He's a child."

"He's bigger than you are. There are a lot of juveniles perpetrating crimes these days."

Victoria looked unimpressed. "I read the newspapers. I know what goes on other places. But I also knew some of Charlie's personal history. That's one thing about small towns. Everybody pretty much knows everybody else's business. From what I'd heard, it seemed to me he needed a break."

"And you decided to give him one?"

"To try, anyway."

For some reason, her explanation appeared to disturb him. But before Victoria could ask why, he said abruptly, "He lives with his sister?"

"That's right."

"You said he'd had a hard time. Don't they get along?"

"It's not that. Pam means well, but she's only twenty-one and she's had some problems of her own."

"She's divorced?"

"Separated."

"And Charlie and his brother-in-law don't get along?"

"That's putting it mildly. It's one of those situations with no easy answer. Will and Pam married young, and neither one is very mature. Will has always had a bad temper, but until Charlie came to live with them, he managed to keep himself under control. He just isn't equipped to deal with a teenager like Charlie, who's still working out his own anger over his father's desertion and his grief over his mother's death. It's sad. For all three of them. I think family counseling would help, but Will won't go, and so far, Pam's been afraid to press him."

A glint of some strong emotion darkened Dare's eyes. "I take it from what Charlie said, his brother-in-law was cheating on his sister?"

He didn't miss much, she realized. "Yes."

"And Charlie found out and wrecked the guy's van to pay him back?"

She frowned. "Where did you hear that?"

His expression turned bland. "Your neighbor must've mentioned it."

She shook her head ruefully before her expression sobered. "I can just imagine what else she said. But regardless of what Will Craig claims or Doris believes, Charlie said he didn't do it—and I believe him."

Dare steepled his fingers. "But a judge didn't?"

"No."

"So Charlie spent some time at a juvenile facility, got behind in school and that's why you're tutoring him," he summarized. "Why didn't you tell me that when I asked you why he needed help with his schoolwork? Why all the bull about a transportation problem?"

She felt the telltale heat rush into her cheeks but ignored it. "It wasn't your business."

"Wrong," he said flatly. "For the time I'm here, where it concerns people you're actively involved with, I need to know what's going on. Domestic disputes are always ugly. What if Charlie had another go-round with his brother-in-law and the guy showed up here looking for him?"

Her chin came up. "It wouldn't be anything new. Since you're so well-informed, you must already know Will wasn't precisely thrilled when I stood up for Charlie at his hearing. We've had a few . . . discussions since then, but I'm certainly not afraid of him."

He rolled his eyes. "You're not afraid of anything, as far as I can tell. That doesn't mean you shouldn't be."

Victoria stared at him in amazement. *But I am,* she almost blurted out. *I'm afraid of lots of things.*

She was afraid of him, and of the way he made her feel, restless and impatient, longing for something she didn't understand. And she was afraid of herself and that Aunt

Alice had been right when she'd warned against the wildness in Victoria's blood. She was afraid she'd do something
reckless that would change her life forever.

But most all, she was even more afraid she wouldn't.

Yet she said nothing. There was nothing to say. And even
if there was, Dare was not the man to say it to.

She drained her ice tea glass and nodded. "Point taken.
Anything else?"

He glanced at his wristwatch. "I guess I better see about
getting that window replaced before it gets much later. Also,
you might want to put together a shopping list. I thought
we'd make a run to the grocery store tomorrow. The cupboards are getting pretty bare."

"Okay."

To her surprise, he continued to sit, staring moodily into
his glass. "There is one other thing." For once, he sounded
uncharacteristically diffident. "The thing is, I just came off
a tough assignment. I've been thinking about it, and I guess
I may've been acting a little rough around the edges."

Stricken, Victoria stared at his bent head. Oh, dear. It almost sounded as if he was . . . apologizing. The realization
set off a jangle of alarm. If she found him attractive when
he was being difficult, what would happen if he decided to
be nice?

It didn't bear considering.

Abruptly, she found her tongue. "Don't worry about it.
Your—your edges are fine. Really."

He looked up, his gaze meeting hers. "Thanks, but we
both know that isn't quite true. So why don't I just say I'll
try to be a little less abrasive in the future—okay?"

Clearly, the only ladylike response was the one she gave.
"Okay."

To her consternation, he smiled. Heaven knew, it only
lasted a second, but it was one terrific smile, a little lop-
sided, a little rueful, revealing even white teeth, a groove in

one cheek—and more sex appeal than an entire chorus line of Chippendale dancers. "Great."

Her wayward heart skipped a beat.

Victoria stifled a groan. Lord help her. She'd need a miracle to make it to September.

Six

There was normal, ordinary, civilized grocery shopping.

And then there was grocery shopping with Dare Kincaid.

The difference, Victoria decided the next day, as she stared at the overflowing contents of their shopping cart, had mostly to do with quantity.

In the former, one purchased what one needed.

In the latter, the prevailing philosophy appeared to be if a little would do, a lot was better.

In the interest of peace, she hadn't said a word when he plucked a package of noodles large enough to feed several small European countries from the shelf. Nor had she commented when he selected a box of cereal so huge, it surely held Iowa's entire corn crop. She kept silent through his acquisition of two loaves of bread, an economy package of ziti, a tub of ricotta, an enormous can of coffee, a fistful of garlic cloves, a pound of fresh mushrooms and a watermelon the size of a beach ball.

But when he tossed what had to be the entire Atlantic fleet's limit of tuna fish into the cart, she couldn't stay silent. "Excuse me . . . Dare?"

Since he'd forged ahead to compare the nutritional labels on a large box of wild rice against an equally big one of white, it was a moment before he answered. "What?" He dropped both boxes into the cart as she came abreast of him.

"Did you invite the town to dinner and forget to tell me?"

He grabbed a giant-size package of spaghetti and looked over at her. "Nope."

"Then what are we going to do with this much food?"

"I don't know about you, but I'm planning to eat it."

It was what she'd been afraid he'd say. Her stomach knotted, but not from hunger. "You may not have noticed," she said carefully, "but I'm not exactly a...gourmet cook."

A flicker of something suspiciously like amusement flashed in his eyes. "Don't worry about it."

"But—"

"I'll take care of it."

She slanted him a look, not certain she'd heard him right. "Really?"

"Sure. I know my way around a kitchen."

She wondered why she was surprised. The man was like a foreign country. The scenery was spectacular, the view terrific, but it was hardly a news flash that she didn't understand the customs or speak the language.

He urged her along with a touch of his hand. "You don't have to look so startled. A lot of men can cook."

"Yes, I know, it's just..." Just what? That once again she was reminded she knew little about him except that he apparently had a thing for tuna fish, looked better in jeans than any man had a right to and would be out of her life in a week?

She refused to let herself dwell on why she found that last thought so disturbing. "Where are you from?"

The simple question appeared to put him on edge. "Right now?"

"Yes."

"Southern California."

Well, that narrowed it down to a few hundred square miles. "Is that where you grew up?"

"No." His face took on a grim look that made it clear it wasn't something he wanted to discuss.

In the interest of peace, Victoria changed the subject. "So how did you learn to cook?"

Incredibly, his expression grew even blacker. "My mother wasn't around much when I was a kid. It was either fend for myself or go hungry."

"But... what about the rest of your family?"

"There isn't any," he said flatly.

"But everybody has somebody—"

"No." He stopped and turned her toward him with his hand on her arm. "Everybody doesn't," he said bluntly. "*You* don't. So just drop it, okay?" Not waiting for an answer, he reached an arm around her and grasped the cart handle, trapping her between it and him. Then he started forward, leaving her no choice but to do the same.

Victoria hardly noticed. She was too busy trying to square his hard-bitten persona with the bleak look she'd seen in his eyes a second before he'd turned away. It was a look she'd seen before—from Charlie. It bespoke a hurt that was black and ugly from being buried too deep and too long. And a vulnerability that was all the more striking given the source.

She tried to tell herself she was imagining things. It would certainly be understandable, considering the effect he had on her. For example, having him close the way he was right now, his hip bumping hers, his hand planted possessively on the small of her back, made her feel funny. On edge, as if all of her senses had gone haywire and turned hypersensitive.

It was similar to the way she'd felt the night she drank too much champagne on the cruise ship to celebrate Mr. and

Mrs. Melon's fiftieth anniversary. Her head had been as light as a helium balloon, her body had tingled and there had been an unfamiliar ache in the vicinity of her navel. She'd been appalled, intrigued, exhilarated and befuddled all at the same time.

The next morning she'd been sick.

Well, that ought to tell you something.

What? That alcohol wasn't for her and neither was Dare? That was hardly a brilliant deduction. A woman didn't reach thirty without having a clear picture of herself. She knew what she was: small, unassuming, average-looking, with stick-straight hair and skinny legs. All the things that had come naturally to the other girls when she'd been growing up, how to dress and fix her hair, how to flirt and talk to boys, still eluded her. About the best that could be said was she had clear skin and all her teeth, was well-read, cared genuinely about people and was an excellent teacher.

As Dare had already demonstrated, those were hardly traits to inspire passion in a man. Still, that didn't mean she didn't fantasize about it. She was only human, after all, and possessed of what Aunt Alice had always called an overdeveloped sense of curiosity. She'd done her share of wondering what it would be like to be swept up in a pair of brawny arms, her body molded against two-hundred-plus pounds of raw masculinity, her breasts crushed against a hard, sculpted chest, her lips claimed by a hot, chiseled mouth...

"Victoria?" Dare's mouth tickled her ear and his breath brushed her cheek as he leaned close.

She jumped a foot. Her traitorous hormones banded together to give a wistful little moan. Heat climbed into her cheeks as for one horrible moment she imagined he'd read her thoughts. She swallowed. "What?"

"You know those two?" He jerked his head a fraction of an inch to his right.

She was so unstrung, it was a second or two before she could focus. A young couple stood at the opposite end of the aisle. The man was big, with short brown hair, a beefy face and ruddy skin; the woman was tall, an attractive blonde with a world-weariness that made her seem years older than she really was.

Although their voices were pitched too low to make out their exact words, it was clear the pair was arguing. His face was red, his eyes narrowed, his entire body tense; her hands were on her hips and her mouth was set in an obstinate line.

"It's Pam and Will Craig," Victoria said as the couple's voices started to rise.

"Damn it, Pammy! If you'd just listen to what I'm saying—"

"Why should I?" Pam Craig responded. "It's not as if you're going to change, Will. It's always like this. You say one thing and then do exactly what you want. No matter how I feel! I really think we ought to see a counselor—"

"I told you, we don't need any damn counselor! We can work our problems out ourselves." His voice turned wheedling. "If you'd just let me move back in, I promise things would be better..."

Pam gnawed on her lower lip. "I don't know. Miss Cooper says that for Charlie's sake—"

"Dammit, it always comes down to your brother and that interfering teacher! What about us, Pammy? What about me? What about what I want?"

"I don't know! I honestly don't know." Her face twisted with misery, Pam started to back away.

Will reached out and grabbed her by the wrist. "Hey, come back here! I'm talking to you!"

At that moment, Charlie came through the swinging door at the back of the store. Caught in the middle of tying his apron on, he paused for only the barest instant, then tossed the swath of green fabric aside and leaped to his sister's assistance. "Let go of her!" he cried.

"Oh, dear," Victoria said. She ducked beneath Dare's arm, eluding him as he tried to restrain her, and bolted down the aisle.

Will turned on Charlie, all of his accumulated frustration roaring to life. "Back off, you little twerp!" he snarled, one big hand closing into a threatening fist.

"That's enough!" Victoria's voice rang out as she whipped around Will and thrust herself between him and Charlie. She drew herself up to her full height and tossed him her best teacher look. "Stop that this instant! You ought to be ashamed of yourself."

Will's face turned scarlet. "*You.* I should've known you'd turn up, interfering as usual. Didn't you listen the last time? This doesn't concern you! This is my family, my business—not yours. So butt out—before you get what's coming to you!"

"I'd be happy to," Victoria answered tartly, her face pale but determined. "As soon as you quit threatening children and start acting your age."

"What's it take to get you to back off? Don't you pay attention? I warned you—"

"Why not try warning somebody your own size for a change?" Dare's voice was quiet but deadly as he moved up behind the younger man.

Will twisted around, a scathing retort on his lips as he prepared to deal with this new aggravation. His fists bunched aggressively, he raised his arm, only to falter as he found that as big as he was, he had to look up to stare into Dare's cold gray eyes. He dropped his hands and took a hasty step back. "Who the hell are you?"

"That's Miss Cooper's husband, you dweeb," Charlie said sarcastically. Will ignored the boy. So did Dare. His body singing with controlled aggression, his attention was all for the younger man as he stepped into the space Will had just vacated. "Who I am is somebody who's going to give you a lesson in manners if you don't clear out of here in the next thirty seconds.''

Will spat a word so crude, Victoria gave an involuntary gasp.

Dare's expression didn't change, although a nerve in his jaw ticked to life. "That'll cost you, pal. Now you've got fifteen seconds.''

Will may have been a hothead, but there was nothing wrong with his instinct for self-preservation. Sputtering with anger, spouting expletives in an effort to save face, he nonetheless turned on his heel and stormed away.

Charlie and Pam watched him go with conflicting expressions, Charlie's gleeful, Pam's a mix of longing, confusion and sadness.

Victoria stared at Dare with wonder.

Dare stared back, his face grim. "I should've known you weren't safe to let out of the house,'' he murmured, so softly only she could hear.

Louder, with a polite nod of acknowledgment, he said, "Mrs. Craig, Charlie. If you'll excuse us?''

He reached out, snagged Victoria's hand and started back toward their cart. "Come on, *sweetheart*. Let's pay for this stuff and get the heck out of here. It appears you need a refresher course on the various applications of rule number seven.''

Victoria wasn't sure when it first dawned on her that Dare was as angry with himself over the incident with Will as he was with her.

The first hint came on the way home, as she sat next to him in her cramped little Volkswagen, which was stuffed so full of groceries, it bulged like a Thanksgiving turkey. It occurred to her, as she stared at Dare's grim face, took note of his unyielding manner and listened politely to the promised lecture on the rules, that perhaps he was overreacting a trifle.

That opinion gained strength when they finally reached the house and she witnessed his elaborate security routine. Instructing her to duck down on the seat, he drove past the house, then doubled back, scrutinizing the yard and garage long and hard before he parked. He hustled her to the door, keeping her behind him as they moved inside and he inspected the kitchen. Then he stashed her in the pantry while he secured the rest of the house. As she stood contemplating jars of pickles and preserves, Victoria decided he was doing it up a bit thick.

After that, she couldn't help but notice the grim-faced way he sorted through the mail, or miss his terse, impatient manner when he called the marshal's office in Billings to ask if there had been any "developments."

By the time they finished eating the delicious dinner he'd fixed, she'd come to the conclusion that his reaction to the run-in with Will was out of all proportion to the actual incident. And that his devotion to duty went way beyond a simple desire to earn his paycheck.

Obviously, there was something else, something more, driving him. The wonder was that it hadn't dawned on her before, she realized, thinking back on the past week. All the clues had been there. From the way he'd brazenly let himself in when she wasn't home, to his telling Doris they were married, to the way he'd gone overboard on home improvements, his actions spoke of a single-minded commitment to her safety that common sense dictated went way beyond his job description.

Her only excuse for not seeing it sooner was that she'd been off balance from the moment she set eyes on him, a condition that hadn't improved with the passage of time. Still, she should have realized long before now that his conduct wasn't standard procedure.

Only one question remained in her mind, but it was a big one.

Why? Why was it so important to him? What had happened in the past that made him so determined to take on such a large responsibility for himself?

The one thing that seemed clear was that he wasn't about to volunteer the information. If she wanted to know, she was going to have to ask. And while it might very well make him angry, and he'd most likely brush her off as he had every other time she'd asked a personal question, she still had to try. As Aunt Alice had often said, nothing ventured, nothing gained.

Gathering her courage, she set her fork on her empty plate, sat back and said into the silence, "Thank you. That was wonderful." She wasn't exaggerating. He'd fixed chicken baked in a cream sauce and served over wild rice, with a tossed green salad and rolls. It had been delicious.

He polished off the last of his roll. "Not much to it."

"There is for some of us," she said lightly.

He scowled. "You try. That's the important part."

Leave it to Dare to say the unexpected. She sighed, wondering why she was even surprised. "I know you may not want to hear it, but I want you to know that I appreciate what you did at the store. I put you on the spot, and I'm sorry about that. I didn't mean to make your job more difficult."

"But?" he said expectantly.

She looked at him quizzically.

"You didn't mean to make my job more difficult but?" he prompted.

A rueful smile tugged at the corners of her mouth. "*But* I couldn't stand by and let Will take his temper out on Charlie," she said after a moment. She cocked her head. "Am I that predictable?"

"Trust me—predictable is *not* the word I'd use to describe you." His tone was laced with irony, but there was no rancor in the words.

Again, it was the last thing she expected him to say. "You should talk." The man had more facets than a diamond, more angles than a compass and more layers than an onion.

"What's that supposed to mean?"

"Did you really hijack that plane in South America?" It had been bothering her for days.

"Where'd you hear about that?"

"The newspaper."

"Yeah? Well, don't believe everything you read. If I'd commandeered that plane, Mendelez would be walking around free and I'd be in jail. My job doesn't put me above the law."

She dropped her napkin on her plate, stood and began to clear the table, ferrying dishes to the counter next to the sink.

"Then how did you get the plane diverted?"

He stood, as well, and carried his own plate to the sink. "Persuasion. That's mostly what tracking fugitives is all about—persuading people to do the right thing. In this case, I got lucky. Mendelez normally traveled by private plane, but his was in for service and I got a tip he'd arranged for a charter. It was a last-minute deal. Turned out the pilot had a brother who'd died from a cocaine overdose, so it was just a matter of convincing him to do the right thing. That, and letting the guys on the other end know we were coming."

It had to have been more complicated than that, but the fact that he was actually talking to her was what was important to Victoria, not the details. "Why did the media imply what they did then?" She put the stopper in one side of the big double sink, squirted in some liquid soap and began to fill the basin with hot water.

Dare transferred leftovers into plastic containers, his face taking on a cynical cast. "Because it sells. Reporting that a fifty-year-old pilot decided to do a good deed and change his flight plan isn't nearly as dramatic as suggesting a U.S.

marshal seized a jet by waving a gun around at thirty thousand feet."

She thought about it for a moment as she finished scraping plates. She realized he had a point, but there was a troubling note in his voice, an edge of disillusionment, a touch of cynicism, a trace of fatigue.... "Do you like what you do?"

He rolled a knife back and forth in his fingers. "It has its moments."

"Do you ever think about doing something else?"

He shrugged. "Sure." He glanced up, his eyes searching hers. "Haven't you?"

Victoria realized he was trying to shift the focus off himself, but didn't mind. "Absolutely. I think about it a lot—usually on the opening day of school, when I look around at all those young faces and wonder if I'll be able to get through to them. It's only... I'm not sure what else I'd do. The only thing I know how to do is teach. Besides, I love it."

Her frankness appeared to relax him fractionally. "Yeah? Why?" He dropped the knife into the soapy water.

"It's a chance to make a difference. With my kids, I always tell myself that if I can just open their eyes to an issue they've never considered or get them excited about something, then I've given them something they'll always have." She stopped, heat warming her cheeks as she realized how idealistic she must sound—again.

To her relief, however, this time he appeared thoughtful. "That's roughly what the guy who's the Marshals Service program director at FLETC said to me," he said slowly.

Couldn't the government ever give anything a name instead of an acronym? "Fletsi?"

"The Federal Law Enforcement Training Center in Virginia," he said. "They've asked me to teach a few courses, but I don't know..."

"You'd be good at it," she said sincerely.

"Maybe. Maybe not. The transition would be hard. So would getting organized. It's been a long time since I've been in a classroom."

"Did you always want to be a marshal?"

He gave her a long look. "Why all the questions?"

"Why not?" she returned calmly. "I'm curious. After all, you know all about me."

"I suppose you've got a point," he murmured. "So what do you want to know?"

"How did you get started?"

"After high school, I enlisted in the service. I did a stint with the military police, racked up some college credits in police science and eventually joined the Houston Police Department. I'd been with them a while when I got paired with a local marshal who was trying to locate an escaped felon suspected of pulling a string of armed robberies. Jimmy and I hit it off, he convinced me I'd be better off with the Marshals and I wound up spending the next few years as a P.O.D."

She gave him a stern look. "In English, please."

A quicksilver smile flashed across his face, every bit as devastating as the one she'd witnessed the previous day. Victoria felt suddenly unsteady, as if the earth had shifted under her feet.

"A P.O.D. is a plain old deputy," he explained. "Like the ones you talked to in Billings. In addition to working felony fugitive warrants, they're in charge of securing the federal courts, transporting prisoners, overseeing witness and judicial security, that sort of thing."

"And that's what you did in Houston?"

"Uh-huh."

"But not anymore?"

"Not since I started working Overseas Warrants."

"What made you decide to try something different?"

His expression grew remote. "I needed a change."

Her hands stilled in the midst of scrubbing a plate. "Why?" she asked softly.

Their eyes met and for a moment his aloof facade slipped, allowing her a glimpse of what was underneath. As she had been earlier that day, Victoria was stunned by the desolation she saw before he abruptly turned away. She was certain he was going to brush her off, but he surprised her by saying, "Jimmy died."

"Your friend?"

"That's right."

"I see." She thought back to what she'd read in the newspaper, about how Dare had been commended for bravery after he, another marshal and a witness had been ambushed. With an intuition she didn't question, she knew his friend Jimmy was the marshal who'd died during that incident. It was also clear that the subject was still painful for him, and that if she pressed, it would be the end of the conversation.

"I'm sorry," she said softly. "It's hard losing someone you love. Particularly when you don't have other family. I've always thought it's the little things that are the worst. Like knowing there isn't a soul in the world who knows you prefer peas to carrots. Or that you love snowstorms. Or who remembers when it's your birthday."

Dare looked at her, the strangest expression on his face. "Yeah," he said gruffly, drying the clean plate she handed him and putting it up in the cupboard. He was quiet for a moment before he said, "Is that how it was for you when your aunt died?"

"Yes. Aunt Alice was strict, overprotective, and I suppose some of her standards were better suited to the nineteenth rather than the twentieth century, but I always knew she loved me. When she died, I felt ... alone."

"What about your parents?"

"Oh, I don't remember my mom, and my dad...well, he was in the Air Force and was gone a lot. He was more out of my life than in by the time he crashed his plane when I was ten.''

Dare put another dish away and began drying silverware, avoiding her gaze. ''My old man walked out on my mother and me when I was ten.'' The words were said flatly, as if to discourage comment and Victoria sensed it was not information he'd volunteered often in his life.

She struggled not to show her surprise he'd shared even that much. Touched by his unexpected trust, she scrubbed a pot, rinsed it and set it in the drainer before she said carefully, ''That must have been hard for you.''

''I did all right. It was my mother who never got over it. She died when I was eighteen. The doctors said it was pneumonia, but I always knew the truth. She quit caring whether she lived or died after that bastard broke her heart.''

The words were all the more powerful for the absolute lack of emotion with which they were uttered. Shocked, Victoria looked up to find him looking at her for her reaction. She pursed her lips and began to scrub the last item left, a baking dish, struggling to keep her dismay from showing on her face.

Eight years. Eight years from the time his father left to when his mother passed away. It was a long time. A long time for a woman to mourn for a broken marriage when she had a child to raise. A long time for a child to spend with a mother bent on grieving herself to death.

Victoria contrasted it with her own experience with Aunt Alice, who, for all her faults, had been a rock a child could depend on. Aunt Alice had believed firmly in the need for adults to hold to a certain standard of responsibility; despite her conservative nature, she'd never believed in lying down and rolling over. Victoria had grown up knowing that whatever else happened, her aunt genuinely cared about her.

She shivered as she replayed Dare's words: *She quit caring whether she lived or died.*

It couldn't have been an easy way to grow to manhood. She glanced at him, trying to imagine him as a gray-eyed, inky-haired little boy. He would have been big for his age. And responsible even then, she thought slowly. Driven, perhaps, to take on far more than any child should—because there was simply no one else to do it.

Her heart twisted. "I'm sorry," she said, for the second time in not many more minutes.

He shrugged. "Don't be. It was a long time ago."

They finished what was left of the dishes in silence. Yet there was an understanding and an easiness between them that hadn't been there before.

At least, that was true until they reached for the dish towel at the same time and Dare's hand closed over Victoria's instead of the fabric.

Startled, Victoria looked up and found herself staring into the dark gray of his eyes. As she had earlier when he smiled, she experienced that subtle sensation of displacement, as if the room had tilted.

She wanted to touch him, she realized. She wanted to lean close and sift the heavy dark silk of his hair through her fingers. She wanted to sample the different textures of his skin with her parted lips. She wanted to open herself to his kiss, rim his ear with her tongue and do all the other delicious, wicked things she'd heard whispered about over the years.

Then what? the logical part of her mind demanded. Did she really want to make love with him?

Granted, he did something to her hormones that ought to be outlawed, and the glimpse she'd had into his past had touched something deep inside her, made her see him as much more than just a very attractive but difficult man. But did that mean she was ready to follow through and share the most intimate act imaginable with him? And do it here—in her own house?

For all that she'd hoped for a romantic interlude on the cruise, she'd had the sense to plan it to happen somewhere safely at a distance from her real life. When it was over, she'd intended to return to her tame little world and go on with her tame little life, which would have remained untouched.

That wouldn't happen with Dare. He was eating at her table, sleeping under her roof. He'd replaced her door and seen her underwear, for heaven's sake. Long after he was gone, she'd still be surrounded by reminders of him.

He was not the sort of man a sane, sensible woman should let herself care about; he was stubborn and opinionated, he had no roots and a dangerous job. He was hardly the type to settle for a plain, spinster schoolteacher—much less settle down with one. Not that she could imagine him living in a place like Gage, anyway. What on earth would he do for a living?

Yet, for all of that, and most alarming, she liked him.

Granted, he could be abrasive and bossy and abrupt. But he also had a subtle, unexpected sense of humor. He was secure enough in his masculinity to do whatever he damn well pleased, like cooking or cleaning. And as their conversation had revealed, there were depths to him that she longed to plumb—and a loneliness that she more than understood. He'd been kind to Charlie. He'd stood up to Will Craig. There wasn't a doubt in her mind that he'd put his life on the line to save hers.

Is this how she repaid him? By making him have to constantly fend her off? When she wasn't sure herself anymore exactly what it was she wanted?

The answer to that was clear. As was her only course of action. Ignoring the weakness in her knees, she pulled her hand free of his, handed him the towel and forced herself to speak with a lightness at odds with the confusion weighing her heart. "Well…it looks as if we're done. I still have a lot of reading to do, so I suppose I'd better get started. Thank you again for the lovely dinner."

Chin up, she fought to keep her expression serene as she left him standing at the sink and walked quickly out of the kitchen.

It didn't escape her notice that he didn't say a word or make a move to stop her.

Seven

"**T**his it?" Holding a gallon can of paint in each hand, Dare paused in the doorway to Victoria's classroom.

The room occupied a corner on the second floor of a quaint brick building located some two miles from her house. The building itself was fifty years old if it was a day, and smelled of chalk dust and floor wax. It had worn linoleum floors and stairs that sported wooden banisters worn to a satin shine from years of buffing by young hands.

Dare took a look around at the large, airy classroom. Rectangular in shape, a row of high windows marched along the outside wall, overlooking a grassy playing field. Off in the distance, the Rockies rose out of the afternoon haze.

Beyond that, there wasn't much to see. As Victoria had explained on the drive over, she'd already taken down all of her displays and arranged to have the custodian cover the desks and floors with tarps. A tall wooden ladder stood under the windows opposite the door. The blackboards were shrouded in paper and tape, as was the old-fashioned cloakroom, which occupied an entire back corner. Only the sink set in a long Formica counter was uncovered.

All that was left to do was the work.

"I can't believe you have to do this yourself," he commented, setting the cans down next to the door.

Victoria laid down her own load of rags, brushes, rollers and other painting paraphernalia. "The budget only stretches so far. School districts are struggling to make ends meet all over the country." She smiled. "I read about a principal in Massachusetts who mows the lawn at his school. At least I don't have to do that."

"You bought the paint."

She shrugged. "It's not much."

"I understand you paid for new textbooks last year."

She narrowed her eyes at him, then shook her head. "Doris talks too much," she said firmly. "I think I'll go change into my painting clothes."

He nodded, welcoming the chance for a moment alone as she walked to the far end of the room and disappeared around the cloakroom wall.

It was the need for some distance that had made him agree to this excursion. Ever since dinner last night, when he'd shot off his mouth and said so much more than he'd ever intended to, he'd felt restless and uneasy, as if he'd explode if he didn't find some outlet for the odd restlessness that overwhelmed him.

Part of it, he acknowledged impatiently, stemmed from his awareness of Victoria as a woman—a warm, desirable woman. It had started the night he'd met Charlie, when he'd first seen the fragile beauty hidden beneath her demure hairstyle and ugly dresses and realized the extent of the passion beneath her proper exterior. It was an awareness that had ripened with every passing day, every conversation, every look that passed between them, increasing along with his need to understand her—and an unprecedented desire to explain himself.

It was that last he didn't want to examine too closely. Yet even as he shied away, he knew it was an equal cause of his frustration. Even though he'd been sure he'd long ago put such inclinations to know and be known, to understand and be understood, behind him.

Obviously not. As much as he wanted to deny it, to pretend that it wasn't so, something had changed between them last night. He knew Victoria had felt it, too; she'd been quiet and skittish ever since.

Still, he shouldn't complain, he thought as he stooped down and pried the lid off a can of white paint someone had whimsically labeled Moondust. He picked up a stir stick, wrinkling his nose at the fumes. If he counted the time a felony fugitive named Joe Bob Zimmer had pushed him into the alligator pit at the San Diego Zoo, fairness compelled him to admit he'd had worse assignments.

It was an opinion that underwent a radical change the moment Victoria walked out of the cloakroom.

Gone was the blue and white floral dress she'd arrived in. Now she was wearing a navy T-shirt that deepened the color of her eyes. And shorts. Demure, tasteful, khaki shorts, that were neither too tight nor too short.

Yet suddenly he knew why she wore those long, loose dresses.

It was to prevent a riot.

The woman was all legs; long and lithe, sleek, slim and smooth legs. Legs that were, in a word, gorgeous.

Her breasts were pretty terrific, too. They were soft and round, surprisingly lush beneath her thin cotton shirt. He wondered if she was wearing one of those sheer lacy bras he'd seen on her bed that first day...

"Is something wrong?"

With a guilty jerk, he glanced away. Directing his attention to the job at hand, he discovered he was stirring the paint so fast, it was starting to get a froth on top like whipped cream. Even worse, his pulse was pounding like a jackhammer and his blood was rushing somewhere other than his brain. All of a sudden, it was hard to remember why it was so important to keep her at arm's length.

Hell in a hailstorm. Give him an alligator to wrestle any day. If he didn't get a grip on himself, he was going to make a complete fool of himself. "Nope, nothing's wrong." He poured paint into a pair of trays, handed her one, picked up the other and a roller and strode toward the far wall. "Let's get started."

She gave him a curious look. "Okay."

The next hour was one of the most tortured of Dare's life. Growing up as he had in rented rooms, there hadn't been much call to do a lot of painting. He figured that explained why he'd never realized what a really physical activity it was.

He soon found out. Every time his gaze strayed in Victoria's direction, she was either bent over the paint tray, providing him with an eyeful of taut little fanny or she was stretching to reach some portion of wall, her long legs taut, her breasts jiggling pertly as she maneuvered the roller up and down.

Pure, unadulterated torture. The room, which had felt cool when they started, quickly heated up. He could feel the perspiration bead on his upper lip and trickle down his back. His skin felt too tight and his nerves felt as if someone were rasping on them with an emery board. Even so, he couldn't seem to quit sneaking peeks at her, prompting him to wonder when he'd developed the masochistic streak.

At the moment, she stood poised near the top of the ladder, her body angled sideways as she ran a brush down the inside corner where the walls joined. The pink tip of her tongue was visible as she nibbled on it in concentration. The slightly puckered tips of her breasts were outlined by her shirt.

Dare gave a start as he felt something cold touch his hand. Looking down, he discovered he was gripping the roller by the pad. Paint oozed through his fingers and dripped onto the floor.

With a curse for his overactive libido, he laid the roller down, wiped his hand on a rag and stalked across the room to the hallway.

He had to get out of there, if only for a moment. "Are you sure you locked the front door after we came in?"

Victoria stopped painting. She wiped her forehead with the back of her hand, leaving a smudge of paint behind in her wake, and raised an eyebrow in question. "You saw me do it."

"Just making sure," he said gruffly.

She watched, puzzled, as he took a quick look around as if to make sure the corridor was empty, before he stepped back, shut the heavy door and locked it. Then he walked to the head of the room, pulled his gun free of his waistband, quickly double-checked the clip and laid it gently down on her tarp-covered desk.

Her mouth went dry as he reached for the buttons of his shirt. "What are you doing?" she squeaked, frozen in place on the ladder. Even to her own ears, her voice sounded panicked.

"It's too damn hot," he grumbled, peeling the paint-splattered gray cotton away from his sticky skin and dropping it in a heap next to his firearm.

Her gaze dropped from his face to his chest as if weighted. She'd never thought of the word *beautiful* in conjunction with a man, but he was certainly that; there was no other word to describe the perfect symmetry of his wide shoulders and broad chest, the way his lightly tanned skin stretched taut over a bewildering array of solid muscle, the controlled ripple of strength in his biceps and triceps.

The man was drop-dead gorgeous. And it wasn't just his smoky eyes or the inky sheaf of hair feathered against his neck or even his to-die-for body that drew the eye, although they were all worthy of a second glance.

No, it was the sheer impact of his masculinity. He exuded raw sex appeal the way a teapot gave off steam.

Not that she cared, she reminded herself, forcing herself to stare at his left earlobe. "Why... why did you lock the door?"

"So if anybody tries to get in, I'll have a chance to get to my gun."

"Oh. Good thinking." She swallowed and forced herself to look away from him entirely. "We'd better get back to work." To her consternation, her hand was shaking; she laid her brush down, balancing it on the ladder top and took up her roller, wielding it like a sword as she attacked the wall with fresh vigor.

She chided herself for overreacting. Yet she couldn't seem to stop the little chills of awareness rolling through her; as a result, her rhythm was off, and rather than creating a steady whir with the roller, her painting was as choppy as a biplane with a faulty carburetor.

She felt Dare's eyes on her even before he spoke. "What's the matter?"

She continued doggedly to paint. "Not a thing."

He raised one eyebrow and indicated the section of wall she'd just finished. "Yeah? Well, something's wrong. Either that or you forgot to tell me you're going for that popular look, nouveau pinto pony."

She stopped and leaned back, staring hard at the section of wall before her. Her jaw tightened as she saw the plate-size sections of old beige paint she'd missed, creating a decidedly splotched effect. "Don't worry about it. I'll catch it on the second coat."

"This is one-coat-guaranteed paint, remember?"

"Look—" she twisted on the ladder, in no mood to debate with him "—I said I'd take care of it and I will!" Her elbow knocked the upper support in her agitation, sending the paintbrush flying. She grabbed for it—and overbalanced. With a panicked cry, she began to fall.

Dare dropped his roller, leaped toward her and plucked her from the air. Hauling her against his chest, he staggered back under the impact, only to catch his foot in a wrinkle in the tarp.

Later, when he recalled that moment, he could never remember hitting the floor. Thought shut down. Feeling took over.

He was kissing her before they reached the ground.

His body cushioned their fall. He felt no pain, only a fierce pleasure; Victoria fit against him as if she'd been made-to-order. He felt the rightness of holding her down deep in his bones.

His hand found her hair. Bobby pins flew, releasing a rain of pale gold that felt like liquid sunshine against his fingers. He breathed in the scent of her, a delicate mixture of apricot soap and summer flowers. The force of his mouth parted her lips. He heard her gasp, felt her arms lock around his neck. A haze of white-hot heat washed through him at her display of eagerness. A low savage sound tore from his throat. He thrust his tongue into her mouth in a kiss that was hard and deep.

He was burning up. He twisted, rolling her beneath him, seeking the cradle of her pelvis, kissing her now in an unabashed simulation of the sex act. His entire body seemed to expand as he settled his hips between her thighs. She whimpered. He felt the hard bead of her nipples against his chest. The thin cotton barrier of her shirt was suddenly unacceptable. He slid his hand under the hem. Her abdomen was taut and as smooth as brushed satin. He reached up and covered a lace-covered breast with his palm. So soft. He circled her nipple with his thumb. So firm.

She whimpered again, pushing herself against him. "Dare—" Her tongue lashed his, then slid across his lower lip and shyly tasted the inside of his mouth. She was shaking, caught in a fever to match his own. Her arms tightened around him. Her fingers gripped his hair. He pressed against her and her body bowed as she pressed back, holding on to him for dear life.

This wasn't just a kiss anymore. It was a prelude to making love.

The thought brought him up short. *Making love?* What the hell was he thinking? He'd never made love in his life. With anybody. He'd had sex. Great sex. Safe sex. Mature, consenting-adult, I-scratch-your-itch, you-scratch-my-itch sex. Sex he was always careful to preface with a blunt talk about how he was not in the market for any emotional ties.

Yeah, right. Somehow, he seemed to have forgotten that little speech this time. And no matter how hard he tried, he couldn't imagine Victoria clambering up off the floor and thanking him casually for the tumble when they were finished. Hell. This was a woman who'd given up living in Paris to look after her persnickety old aunt. Who was willing to take a chance on jail rather than risk hurting a hard case like Charlie. He had a feeling the whole concept of casual, feel-good sex would go right over her head.

Even worse, she was probably a virgin.

Good God. Was that even possible in this day and age?

The whole pattern of thought didn't take more than a handful of seconds. He wished it had taken longer. God knew he didn't want to stop.

Great, Kincaid. Real admirable. Keep this up and for your next assignment Arizzo might let you guard a Catholic girls' school.

With a groan, he tore his mouth away. He forced his eyes open, then wished to hell he hadn't. Victoria's hair was a golden nimbus around her head. Her lips were moist, swollen from his kisses and pouty as she gave a little moan of protest at his abrupt absence. Her lashes, dark in contrast to the gilt halo of her hair, lifted to reveal summer-sky eyes, hazy with need.

Holy Saint Seraphina. Had he ever really thought she was prim? He must need his eyes examined. Better yet—how about his head?

"Victoria—" As if operating independent of his brain, his fingers reached out and he swept a silky strand of hair back from her cheek, luxuriating in the creaminess of her skin.

She stared up at him, her desire for him as easy to read as if it were being broadcast on a teleprompter. Before he realized her intention, she raised her head and pressed her lips to the side of his throat. "Don't stop," she whispered.

He wanted to punch someone. He wanted to punch *himself*.

"This is a mistake." His voice, thick with frustrated lust, came out harsher than he intended.

She stilled. For a moment, the only sound in the room was their labored breathing. He felt her take a deep, shuddery breath. Then, very slowly, she eased back down. Her eyes locked on his. She moistened her lips. "What—what did you say?"

He hoisted himself up, rolled sideways so that he was sitting up, his back angled to her. He hunched his shoulders. "I'm the last guy on earth you want to get involved with," he said flatly. "Come next week, and I'm out of here."

Out of the corner of his eye, he watched her sit up, her movements slow, as if it hurt her to move.

He could sympathize with that, he thought, coming to his feet in an effort to lessen the strain on his jeans. Restless, he paced away, trying to dissipate some of the sexual energy coursing through him.

"I'm old enough to make my own decisions." Her voice was muted, but surprisingly calm.

He relaxed a fraction and turned to face her. She was on her knees, tucking in her T-shirt, avoiding his gaze.

He ran a hand through his hair, exasperated at the way his body tightened even more when she raised her arms to smooth back her hair, giving him a perfect view of the aroused points of her nipples. "You may be old enough in years, but you sure as hell haven't had enough experience to know what you're doing."

Her head jerked up. The color faded from her cheeks. Too late, he saw the hurt in her eyes. Abruptly, he realized she'd taken what he'd said as a comment about her ability to please him, rather than his very real concern that her relative innocence would result in her getting hurt.

He opened his mouth to set her straight, then slammed it shut again. So what if he prized her honest, unschooled passion more than he'd ever valued another woman's polished technique? So what if her innocence appealed to some primitive urge he'd never known he had? So what if he couldn't remember when a woman had made him so hot?

It was better she never know. As much as he despised himself for causing her pain, the truth was she'd be better off giving him a wide berth.

He remembered the first day in her kitchen. What was it he'd told himself? Something about no warm-and-fuzzy stuff, no Kodak moments? It had been damned good advice.

Now all he had to do was remember it.

He shuttered his gaze, steeling himself as Victoria hid her hurt away, gathering her composure along with her hairpins. By the time she climbed to her feet, she'd managed to wrap herself in an air of quiet dignity. He felt an unwanted twinge of admiration.

Her chin came up. "You're right. I've never... I mean, how foolish of me to think—" She stopped, swallowing hard. "Well, you know." With an eloquent shrug, she picked up her fallen roller, clutched it in one unsteady hand, turned and climbed back up the ladder. "If we're going to finish this today, we'd better get to it."

Dare stared at the delicate line of her back, then stooped to retrieve his own roller.

Why the hell, he wondered, did doing the right thing feel so wrong?

* * *

What was left of the afternoon passed in near-total silence. They finished painting, cleaned their equipment and left it for the custodian to put away. Then they washed up at the classroom sink, Victoria changed into her dress and Dare put his shirt back on and they set off for home in the car.

The drive seemed to take forever. Victoria stared fixedly out the window. She was peripherally aware of Dare, who was all business, eyes watchful, body tense, his professional demeanor back in place.

He didn't look any happier than Victoria felt.

She told herself she didn't care. She was having enough trouble maintaining a calm facade without worrying about his feelings. As long as she kept her attention on the scenery, she could hold the worst of her hurt at bay. By the same token, instinct warned that if she gave his proximity more than a passing thought, she'd lose control and give voice to the misery lodged inside her like a stone.

She could imagine his disdain if she let that happen. The only person who'd be more appalled was her. She could fall apart later, she promised herself. Just as soon as they got home. She would retreat to the sanctuary of her bedroom, lock her door and let loose. For now, she had to maintain.

But it wasn't easy. Not with him so close.

And not when she knew she had nobody but herself to blame for what had happened.

Dare had made it painfully clear from the moment they met that he didn't find her physically attractive. Why, they'd barely said hello that first day before he'd referred to her as a "dinky little blonde," which could hardly be construed as a compliment. Nor had he said or done anything in the intervening days to make her think he'd changed his opinion.

Why, in order to get him to kiss her, she'd literally had to fall off a six-foot ladder and knock him to the ground. And even so, once he'd recovered from the shock—and an initial surge of lust she'd decided was no more than an understandable reaction to *her* fevered desire for *him*—he'd put a swift halt to things.

Yet despite her injured pride and her genuine hurt over his rejection, her only real regret was that they'd stopped. For once, she didn't care about doing the tame, safe thing.

Because, after all her imagining, after all her speculation, she no longer had to wonder what passion was. Finally, she knew.

It had been a bit of a shock, she had to admit. It wasn't neat and tidy, a poetic fusion of souls. It wasn't hearts and flowers, violin music and pretty chiming bells.

Instead, it was hot and hungry, an explosion of sensation almost too intense to bear. It was giving yourself up, being stripped bare, having all of your secret, inner places exposed. It was raw and primitive, a little sweaty. It was scary, exciting, overwhelming.

It was heavenly, and she'd wanted more.

"Victoria?"

"What?"

"Do you know whose car that is?"

She looked up with a start to find they were approaching her house. The vehicle in question was a dark green van, parked in front of Mrs. Vonnegut's. "It belongs to Doris's daughter, Carrie," she told him. "She lives in Livingston, but she tries to come by once or twice a month so that Doris can spend some time with Amy, her two-year-old."

"You sure?"

She looked at the car seat visible in the back seat. "Yes."

He pulled into the driveway, only to murmur a swearword as he saw Charlie waiting for them on the front porch. "What's he doing here?"

For a moment, she didn't have the slightest idea, and then she realized it was Tuesday. "We have a lesson," she said tiredly. She couldn't believe she'd forgotten again. Sighing, she closed her eyes to try to pull herself together.

When she opened them a moment later, she found herself staring at the familiar interior of her garage. What's more, Dare had come around and was holding the car door open for her. Feeling foolish to be caught with her eyes closed like some overwrought child, she climbed out, careful not to brush against him as he took up his usual position a half step in front and to the side of her and they walked toward the house.

They had just stepped onto the porch when a shrill scream split the summer twilight. Along with Dare and Charlie, Victoria jerked around at the sound, her attention drawn across the way to Doris's porch, where Carrie Vonnegut Taylor stood, her face a mask of fright. She clutched her mother's arm with one hand, her gaze riveted on the street.

Victoria turned, and immediately understood the young mother's distress. In the middle of the road toddled Carrie's daughter, Amy, her chubby little legs churning as she chased after a scraggly orange cat. Barreling down the road directly toward her was a souped-up old car. The vehicle had a headlight out and appeared to be filled with several teenagers who had the stereo turned on full blast. The car raced down the narrow, shadow-pocked road, speakers blasting, its occupants clearly unaware of the child in their path.

Equally oblivious to the fast-approaching danger, Amy grabbed for the elusive cat, which promptly bounded out of reach. With a wail of frustration, the little girl lost her balance and, to her audience's added horror, plopped down in the middle of the street.

"Oh, my word—"

"Good heavens—"

"Dear God!"

Frozen with horror, everyone on both porches spoke at once, except for Dare, who took one all-encompassing look and said tersely to Victoria, *"Stay here."*

Then he vaulted over the porch railing and set off across the yard at a dead run.

Eight

"**W**ow! He's pretty fast for an old guy."

Charlie's excited comment jarred Victoria out of a momentary paralysis. She hurried to the railing, her heart pounding as she watched Dare race away.

She felt the early-evening air against her face. She was peripherally aware of Charlie moving up beside her, of Doris and Carrie saying something from across the way, of her own uneven breathing, before she tuned out everything around her.

Just as Charlie had said, Dare ran with incredible swiftness for such a big man. But he was no match for the car, which continued to approach at a high rate of speed, its front bumper gleaming dully in the dusky light. It was so close, Victoria could feel the bass boom of the radio in her bones.

She couldn't imagine how he could possibly hope to outrace it when, suddenly, he put on a burst of speed. Clapping a hand over her mouth to stifle a scream, Victoria watched in horror as he swept in practically under the vehicle's tires and snatched up the child. She rocketed onto her toes, lending him her strength, as he launched himself toward the far side of the road.

He wasn't going to make it. The thought unfurled in her mind like a funeral banner as the car overran the space Dare had occupied only seconds earlier. Time seemed to slow. She waited, her need to know that Dare and Amy were all right approaching desperation.

Finally, in a flash of chrome and rusty paint, the car flashed past. And there, on the far side of the street, tumbling across the neighbor's lawn, was Dare, Doris's grandchild cradled protectively in the curve of his arms.

He rolled to a stop. And didn't move, causing Victoria's heart to stop. And then he sat up and gave himself a little shake, as if testing to make sure everything was still working. He looked down and said something to the toddler on his lap. The little girl promptly gave a howl and began to scream for her mother. A chorus of relief went up from Doris and Carrie, who zoomed down the stairs like a pair of pebbles hurled from a slingshot.

Victoria didn't move. Not because Dare had told her to stay put, but because she couldn't. Her legs felt like two pieces of limp spaghetti, and the rest of her oxygen-starved muscles were weak and trembling.

He'd done it. He was all right. The child was all right. Everything was fine.

Except…he could have died. The idea slammed into her, setting off a ripple of emotions: thankfulness that he hadn't, admiration for his courage, anger at the chance he'd taken, anguish at the thought of going on without him if he hadn't made it.

The last thought was most disturbing. It was so foolish. After all, she certainly had no claim on him. It wasn't as if they really were married, or anything. They'd only shared a kiss, and to date, it had caused her as much anguish as pleasure.

"Are you okay, Miss Cooper?" Charlie asked. In stark contrast to herself, the boy didn't seem the least bit troubled. He sounded excited. And impressed.

She released a pent-up breath and forced herself to breathe normally. "Yes. Of course I am." To her relief, it was almost true. She was only shaking a little.

"That was so cool." Charlie's blue eyes were dark with his enthusiasm. "It was just like in the movies! Tell me the truth—is he really with the CIA? Or the Special Forces, or something?"

She gave an inner sigh, still not comfortable with having to lie. "No."

Thankfully, the teen appeared oblivious to her distress. "Well, he sure doesn't act like any travel agent I ever saw! First he threw himself in front of a bullet—"

"It was a rock, Charlie."

"Yeah, but he *thought* it was a bullet and you're always saying it's the thought that counts. And he made Will back down at the store the other day, and now, today, he saves a baby from a speeding car. Hey, I know—" the boy laughed, all pumped up with nervous energy "—maybe he's Superman!"

"I don't think so, Charlie." As close as Victoria could remember, Superman hadn't risen above a sad and difficult childhood. Nor were his feats of courage performed at the risk of his own life. He didn't swear or lose his temper. He didn't cut his hand on screwdrivers or bleed—at least, not in Victoria's kitchen. He didn't knock himself out securing her house, or eat her cooking without complaint, or act with unexpected kindness toward audacious fourteen-year-olds. He didn't have a kiss so hot it scorched her socks.

Superman was good.

Dare was better.

That was why she loved him.

Victoria went very still. She . . . *loved* him?

She swayed as the enormity of the thought fully registered. Oh, dear. And here she'd thought she was simply suffering from a bad case of lust.

Barely aware of what she was doing, she reached out and grabbed Charlie for support. "Are you sure you're all right, Miss Cooper?" The boy's grin faltered as he turned and got a good look at her face. "You look a little funny."

No, I'm not all right, she suddenly longed to say. *I've gone and done something incredibly foolish.*

She didn't, however. Firmly getting a grip on herself, she squelched the impulse to blurt out her feelings as swiftly as it had sprung up. It was going to be difficult enough, as it was, to explain the situation to Charlie when it ended. She wasn't going to complicate it anymore by making an ill-advised declaration—to anyone. "Of course I am." For once, the lie slipped off her tongue as easily as rain rolling off a rooftop.

"Is it okay if I go join the others, then?" Obviously eager to be in the thick of the action, he gestured to the spot across the street where Doris and Carrie had converged on Dare. Victoria forced herself to smile. "Sure." She started to wave him off, then stopped. "Except—do you mind if we postpone our lesson tonight? After all the excitement, I—I have a touch of a headache."

"No problem."

"We can make it up later."

"Sounds good to me." Unable to contain himself any longer, the youngster leaped the railing in a fair imitation of Dare and loped across the grass.

Victoria watched him go with a surge of fondness. It was so nice to see him minus his usual wary facade, to see him actually look up to someone the way he was starting to look up to Dare. Still, it worried her for the future. When she'd initially suggested the two be friends, it had seemed so unlikely, she hadn't stopped to consider how the boy would feel when the marshal left. Now, it was too late.

She hadn't stopped to consider a lot of things, she thought, with a shaky stab at humor. Topping the list was that she might fall in love with the man passing himself off as her husband.

She took a deep breath and told herself firmly it was a ridiculous idea. That the powerful emotions racing through her had nothing to do with love. They came from unsatisfied lust, from the injury to her pride caused by his rejection, from the struggle between the reckless yearnings of her heart and the prudent course urged by her common sense.

There had to be some explanation other than love.

An elusive memory nagged at her. She searched her mind, until she finally remembered.

Stockholm Syndrome. She'd taught her students about it last year when they'd done a unit on psychology. It was a condition defined as a sudden sense of emotional connection and dependency associated with one's captor. It was usually brought on by stress and enforced reliance.

That had to be it, she decided. Lord knew, the circumstances certainly fit.

That's right, said the little voice in her head. *And if you wish hard enough, maybe you'll wake up tomorrow morning, look in the mirror and discover you're Julia Roberts.*

She sighed. Who was she kidding? What she felt for Dare wasn't some exotic emotional condition. It was love, bright and lucent, illuminating the darkest corners of her heart, as easy to identify as a beacon shining through her. Try as she might to deny it, she couldn't dim the light.

Across the street, Dare climbed to his feet. Rubbing his hip as if to ease a hurt, he handed Carrie her daughter, looking distinctly uncomfortable as mother and child hugged in a fierce embrace, both of them wailing like banshees. Doris anxiously patted her daughter and granddaughter to soothe them, then turned to Dare, clutched gratefully at his hand and began to talk a mile a minute. Charlie stood back, watching and listening to the hubbub around him.

Victoria's gaze settled on Dare. She watched as he shrugged in the familiar, dismissive way he had at something Doris said. Even from this distance, she could see his uneasiness at the fuss the elderly lady was making over him. A wave of tenderness went through her, only to be quickly followed by a surge of anxiety as he took a quick look around and then zeroed in on her.

Even in the poor light, she could see he was assessing her, checking to make sure everything was all right.

That's when she realized she couldn't face him. Not now. Not yet. Not when everything she felt for him was probably written all over her face.

She had to get out of there. Fast.

"You're a hero! A genuine hero!" Mrs. Vonnegut insisted, her voice still shaky from the recent fright she'd had.

"It was no big deal," Dare said. He tried to reclaim his hand, only to find the old lady had no intention of releasing it. "Anybody would've done the same. Really." It was hard, but he forced himself to be civil, although he was in no mood to make small talk. The combined effect of an overdose of adrenaline, Mrs. Vonnegut's insistence on labeling him a hero and the biting awareness that he'd left Victoria unprotected, was having a decided effect. His temper was paper-thin.

"Oh, I don't think so," Mrs. Vonnegut said, not helping matters by contradicting him. "Why, you were already scooping our Amy up when the rest of us were still trying to decide what to do." She turned to Charlie for support. "Wasn't he, Charles?"

"Yeah," the boy agreed eagerly, an unlikely ally. "You were great, Mr. Kincaid! It was so cool! I couldn't believe it when you went flying in front of that car—"

"Exactly!" Mrs. Vonnegut chimed in, not to be out-done. "Why, my heart was palpitating so! I can tell you, it took five years off my life—"

Feeling cross enough to wrestle a grizzly bear as the old lady and the boy continued to chatter, Dare stared across the street at Victoria. She had the strangest expression on her face. Almost as if she were in pain. Or afraid of something.

The thought sent a coil of uneasiness unwinding through him. Frowning, he decided enough was enough. Charlie and Mrs. Vonnegut could do the instant replay without him. He needed to get back to his real job.

He retrieved his hand with a firm jerk. "Excuse me. But Victoria is waiting and—"

"Do you work out?" Charlie inquired.

He could feel his patience disintegrate like a piece of wet tissue. "Yes. Now, like I said—"

"Surely you must run, as well?" Mrs. Vonnegut as-serted. "Why, you're so fast—"

"Like I said—" he raised his voice " —Victoria's waiting on the porch and—"

Mrs. Vonnegut shook her head. "No, she's not."

"She is, too," he countered irritably. *She'd better be.* He glanced at the porch in question to reassure himself.

Victoria was nowhere in sight.

He rounded on Mrs. Vonnegut and Charlie, pinning them in place with a gaze as sharp as an ice pick. "Did either of you see where she went?"

Charlie swallowed, a perplexed crease between his eye-brows. "She was right there."

"I know that."

"She probably just went inside. She said she had a head-ache and asked if we could cancel our lesson tonight. I said fine—"

"Thanks. I'll see you both tomorrow." Too damn mad to care what they thought, Dare left the pair staring after him and charged toward Victoria's house.

Despite his anger, habit made him take a quick circuit of the yard before he stormed up the steps and checked out the porch. Fuming when he found the back door wide open, he strode inside. None of the lights were on. The room was deserted. *"Victoria!"* he bellowed, his temper fueled by a growing sense of alarm.

There was no response. He moved swiftly through the murky kitchen and quickly checked out the first floor, which proved to be as empty as he'd expected. He bounded up the stairs, taking them two at a time. He stalked down the hall, his mouth set in a forbidding line, and threw open her bedroom door.

She was there, her back to him as she stood outlined against the twilight gleaming beyond the window.

The sight of her safe and sound sent a crest of relief crashing through him.

It was swiftly followed by a renewed wave of fury. "Dammit, Victoria! What the hell do you think you're doing?"

She turned, her face shadowed. "Are you all right?"

He brushed off her concern with a wave of his hand, so angry at the scare she'd given him, he could barely get the words out. "I'm fine."

"That was very brave, what you did, going after Amy like that. You could've been killed."

The last thing he wanted to hear was another tribute to his bravery. "I did what I had to," he clipped out. "Which is a hell of a lot more than I can say for you. I told you to wait for me on the porch!"

She hugged herself, her hands clutching her bare arms as if to ward off a chill. "I'm sorry. I—I needed something upstairs."

He couldn't believe it when she turned her back on him again to gaze out the window. *"You* needed?" He was across the room in two strides. "Let me tell you about need! I need to know I can trust you to do what I say. I need to know I can turn my back on you for five seconds without you doing something stupid like charging into an unsecured house! I need to know you're safe, dammit!'' He reached out, intending to tug her around, only to find he'd made a serious mistake as she turned at the same time and the delicious softness of her breast filled his outstretched hand.

With that single touch, desire roared through him like a runaway train at full throttle. It was as if the long, agonizing hours of restraint since their encounter in the classroom had only served to stoke the power of his passion.

He wanted her. More than he had before. More than he'd ever wanted anyone. The thought charged through him in the same instant her nipple beaded against his palm, undeniable proof that she wanted him, too.

And yet nothing else had changed. An involvement between them was still a bad idea.

Yet . . . what harm could one kiss do? One kiss, he promised himself and then he'd put a stop to this, once and for all.

"Victoria." Her name was a whisper as stark as his need, as hot as his blood. He tangled a hand in her hair and tipped back her head, only to freeze when he looked down to find her eyes were silvered with tears. "What is it?"

She looked up into the passion-strained planes of his face and told him the truth. "Don't . . . don't kiss me unless you mean it, Dare. Unless you really want me. Unless you don't intend to stop. Because if you do kiss me, and then you get turned off by my lack of experience again, I don't think—'' a single tear trembled on her lashes ''—I don't think I could stand it.''

She squeezed her eyes shut. The tear traced a glittering path down her cheek, washing away all his well-thought-out intentions, dissolving the wall around his heart.

Victoria didn't cry. Victoria met the world on the point of her proud little chin—or had, until he'd reduced her to this.

With sudden understanding, he realized he'd seriously underestimated the cost to her pride of his previous rejections. The knowledge shattered something deep inside him.

Misinterpreting his silence, she said brokenly, "I know I'm not sexy or particularly pretty or even very young, but—"

"Shh." He pressed his index finger against her lips, her words slicing at him like a lance. Then he gently loosened the death grip she had on the front of his shirt, took her hand and pressed it to the arousal straining his jeans. "Does that feel like I don't want you?"

Startled, she jerked her hand away. "Dare—"

"You only got one part right." He leaned down and kissed her eyes, the curve of her cheek, the corners of her mouth with a tenderness that stole her breath. "You're not pretty. You're beautiful..." Whatever else he might have said was lost as his mouth settled avidly over hers.

There was no mistaking his sincerity. Victoria could feel his hunger in the sudden heat of his skin, in the uneven quality of his breathing, in the quiver of silk-steel muscle as he swept his hands down her back and pulled her urgently against him.

By the time he raised his head, they were both breathing hard. He rested his forehead against hers. "Make no mistake, I want you," he rasped, his voice strained. "But this won't work. I've got a job to do. And just like I said earlier, I'm going to leave next week, which is how I want it. I'm no damn good at relationships. My job... my life... There's no place in either one for commitments—"

"I'm not asking for that. All I want is what you're willing to share with me now." She'd worry about the rest of it later, she told herself.

"Are you sure?"

"*Yes.*" This was her time to live—for once, she wasn't going to miss out because she didn't have the courage to follow her heart's desire.

"We have one other problem."

Victoria's heart lurched painfully. Surely, after such a searing kiss, after she'd bared her soul so painfully, he wouldn't rebuff her now?

"I don't have any way to protect you."

Her relief was so acute, she felt faint. She leaned against him, resting her cheek against his chest, and fought to catch her breath. "I do."

Surprise rippled through him. "You do?"

"Yes. I bought them for the cruise."

He went very still; she could almost feel him thinking. "We're going to have to talk about that cruise," he said after a moment.

She gave a shaky laugh. "Nothing happened. That's why I still have them."

"Yeah? Well, you don't have to sound sorry about it."

He sounded jealous. Even though she knew it was less than admirable, she couldn't contain the bubble of happiness that welled up inside her. She pressed a kiss to the warm notch where his collarbones met, gathered her strength and walked to the closet, where she reached up and pulled a carryall bag from the shelf.

It only took a moment before she handed him a box sealed in cellophane.

"What did you do?" He pulled her close and pressed a series of butterfly kisses to the silky skin of her throat. "Buy the biggest box they made?"

"Aunt Alice always said, 'Better safe than sorry,'" she told him, trembling as his lips whispered over her face.

He urged her against him, bringing them together in a slow, rocking rhythm that was as tantalizing as it was suggestive. A burst of heat went through her at the feel of him, thick and rigid against her belly. She parted her lips for the thrust of his tongue, whimpering at the hot, heady taste of him, plucking feverishly at his shirt. She wanted to be close, bare skin to bare skin. She wanted to feel the curl of hair on his chest against her breasts.

She wanted him inside of her, hot and big and male.

In a motion as old and intuitive as time, she came slowly up onto her toes, measuring him against her body.

Dare groaned. "Slow down, sweetheart." He sketched a line of openmouthed kisses to the satiny skin behind her ear. "I want it to be good for you." He made a low, rueful sound that was almost a chuckle. "Hell, who am I kidding? I just want it to last longer than five seconds . . ."

Victoria laced her hands in his hair and turned to capture his mouth with her own, a little bemused by her own boldness. "Whatever happens will be perfect," she said against his lips. "Because it's you. I've waited so long for you . . ."

Her breathy certainty cut through the last of his restraint. He took a half step back. With hands that shook, he pulled the pins from her hair and combed it with his fingers until it lay against her shoulders, gleaming like early-morning sunlight in the dimness of the room. He brushed her kiss-swollen lips with his fingers and began to slide the buttons of her dress free, peeling back the fabric inch by inch until it bunched at her waist.

He caught his breath. Her breasts were perfect, small creamy globes that strained at the sheer champagne lace of her bra, which he promptly unsnapped and tossed to the floor. The pulse point in his throat leaped; her nipples were pale pink and drawn into tight points that begged for his touch. He pushed her dress to the floor, swallowing as he saw she was wearing nothing more than a scandalous pair of thong bikinis.

He had to touch her. The need blew through him with hurricane force. Bowing his head, he wrapped an arm around her waist and lashed one sweetly pointed nipple with his tongue. At her gasp, he closed his mouth over her and drew sharply, savoring her tightly beaded flesh.

"Oh . . . !" She clutched at his shoulders and hid her face in the silky darkness of his hair as her knees buckled. Sensation flooded her. There was the rasp of his beard-roughened cheek against her tender skin; the steely strength of his arm holding her up; the bunched muscles of his back flexed beneath her palms. There was the wet heat of his mouth, the restrained nip of his teeth; she felt the rhythmic pull from his hollowed cheeks both at her breast and between her thighs, a blazing echo of sensation as real as the stroke of his fingertips.

She heard a voice murmuring, "Yes," over and over again.

Vaguely, she recognized it as her own.

He paused and she looked down. Their eyes met. Hers felt heavy-lidded, weighted with her need for him. His were smoke-dark and fierce, a silver-edged flame. He rose and gave her a hard kiss on the mouth.

"*Yes,*" he answered, voice hoarse. He kicked out of his shoes, tore off his shirt, skinned out of his jeans and briefs. He hooked his hands in the elastic of her panties, his fingers sliding slowly down the length of her thighs, a brand licking her with flame as he pushed the scrap of fabric down until she was free of it.

He straightened, his gaze painting her with heat as it skimmed from the thrust of her trembling breasts, to the nip of her slender waist, to the gentle swell of her hips.

And then he slowly traced the same path with his hands. His thumbs trailed down her midriff, over her navel, across the slope of her belly, through the pale tangle of curls that crowned the heart of her femininity. He rotated his thumb against her, his touch whisper-soft, and felt the melting warmth, the slick wash of her desire.

Her entire body shuddered. "Dare . . ."

He wanted to sink to his knees before her. He wanted to taste her. He wanted to stroke her until she opened to him like a beautiful, exotic flower.

"Dare, please..."

He barely heard her over the roaring in his ears.

Yet he heard enough to register the tremor of panicked shyness in her voice, to remember this was her first time.

Every muscle in his body quivered. He fought for restraint, gritting his teeth as he saw to their protection before he swept her into his arms. He took two steps back and dropped with her onto the bed, his hands tangling in her hair as he rolled her beneath him.

A tremor went through her as he settled into the cradle of her thighs. He was rock-hard and heavy, a solid wall above her. He was taut and velvet-smooth over a dense, unyielding layer of muscle. Excitement twisted through her, edged with an undeniable border of apprehension.

Outside, a breeze whispered through the trees. Light from the rising moon danced across the walls. She could see him clearly, could see the almost savage look on his face as she felt him nudge against her. Her hands bit into his shoulders, her body arched as he slowly eased forward. "Oh," she gasped at that first incredible pressure. "I don't think this is going to work..."

Braced on his elbows, he leaned down and kissed her, his tongue stroking her mouth as he joined their bodies, inch by inch. "Don't think," he whispered back. "Feel." She'd expected pain, and there was some; a burning, brightly flaring hurt, a searing fullness, a dull ache that faded quickly as she opened to his welcome invasion. And then...a flood of impressions. Slick. Smooth. Hot. Big.

And right. So right.

He began a slow, measured withdrawal; Victoria arched her hips in an instinctive urge to bring him back. She framed his face in her shaking hands, meeting him kiss for kiss, on fire with a fierce tenderness, only to cry out against his mouth as he flexed his back and did as she asked, driving into her.

"Victoria..." Her name was a prayer, a need, a gift. He began to move, slow at first, but then faster and faster, harder and harder.

His shoulders were sweat-slick beneath her hands. His weight pressed her into the mattress; she couldn't breathe and she didn't care. Nothing mattered except for Dare, the way he felt against her, around her, inside her, as he lit a fuse that grew shorter with every stroke of his body. Something was stealing up on her, something hot and intense and explosive, and he was the fire that threatened to consume her, the trigger for the series of small explosions that were starting to rush through her, bringing that elusive something closer.

She clutched at him, bowed up off the bed, pressed against him as he thrust more and more powerfully until everything inside her suddenly ignited in a flash point of blinding light, an overload of sensation. Her entire body contracted, and when it did, it drew a cry from Dare that seemed to come from deep inside him, as if he were being turned inside out.

Victoria heard her name on his lips and opened her eyes, in time to see the exultation on his face as he poured himself into her.

And she knew, as she looked up at him, as she raised a trembling hand and rested it against his cheek, that she'd been right to wait—for this time, this moment, this experience—with this man. Whatever else happened, she'd always know, clear to her very soul, how thoroughly she'd been loved tonight.

No one could take that away from her.

Nine

"Hey, buddy." In what had become a morning ritual, Dare opened the door to the little orange tabby.

The feline gave him a reproachful stare before it stalked in with a plaintive yammer, clearly put out at having been kept waiting.

Dare shook his head at the animal's manner. He knew he was up considerably later than usual, a fact reflected by the sun slanting in the windows like a shower of golden arrows. But then, he'd barely slept. He'd been too busy loving Victoria, whom he'd left fast asleep upstairs.

"You've got some nerve giving me a bad time," he told the cat, hunkering down to scratch its chin. "Not after the stunt you pulled last night, playing hard to get with that little girl. You nearly got her killed." He paused. "Hell, you nearly got *me* killed. You know what that would've meant, don't you?"

Completely unaffected by the scolding, the furry beast arched its back and leaned against his shins, rumbling like a cement mixer with a bad muffler.

Dare straightened and stared sternly down at the animal. "No more free lunch, that's what. So make sure you don't do it again." He picked up a bowl of tuna from the counter and carried it over to the door. He set the food down outside, a faint smile touching his mouth as the animal bounded across the room and pounced on it. "Clean up your act, cat," he said softly before he shut the door.

When he turned, he found Victoria standing in the entrance from the hallway, watching him.

He wasn't sure what he'd expected when they first came face-to-face out of bed, but it wasn't this. Their gazes met. An embarrassed flush crept up his neck as he saw the knowing look in her eyes.

"I was getting worried," she said, studying him. "I couldn't imagine how anyone could eat that much tuna without developing gills and fins."

She was naked except for his shirt. Her golden hair was tumbled, her skin sleep-flushed, her lips swollen from the long night of passion they'd shared. She crossed her arms; his mouth went dry as the shirt rose until it barely skimmed the tops of her slim thighs.

"You might as well come clean," she continued softly. "You fed that creature my cream, didn't you?"

Desire twisted through him. He wanted her—again. Even though they'd made love twice more last night, and again in the pearly predawn light only a few hours ago. He wanted to cross the room, slide his hands up under that wrinkled cotton and stroke her smooth, pale skin. He wanted to thrust his tongue into her mouth. He wanted—

Too much. More, he suspected, than was possible. Certainly more than was wise.

With a sudden sense of disquiet, he realized he felt closer to Victoria than he had to anyone in years, maybe ever. The ramifications were alarming. If he had any sense, he'd put a stop to this now. Before she got the wrong idea. Before she got any ideas at all.

"Dare?" The soft inquiry focused his attention on her. He took in the way she had her fingers plaited together, realizing the unfamiliar note he heard in her voice was an edge of uncertainty.

She was nervous, he realized. Afraid, perhaps, of what he was about to say? He hesitated, remembering her vulnerability—and how badly he'd miscalculated it before.

Please. If you stop now, I don't think I could stand it.

Tenderness swept him. Aw, hell. It wasn't as if she was facing some immediate, acute danger. He could handle this. After all, as long as it was only his hormones that were engaged and nothing else, what could it hurt?

He struggled to look nonchalant. "Cream is bad for you," he informed her. "All that cholesterol."

Her fingers slowly untwined. Her shoulders relaxed and she let out her breath. "Ah, I see. You were just doing your job, protecting me?"

"That's right."

She nodded, her expression thoughtful. "And the tuna was to save me from . . . mercury poisoning?"

"You got it."

A smile crept over her face and he found himself smiling back, savoring the playful exchange. There had never been much space for lightness in his life. Like a child with an unexpected confection, he savored the sweetness of the moment.

Still, it seemed as if he ought to say *something*. Just to make sure there were no misunderstandings. "Victoria . . . about last night—"

She padded across the room and pressed a finger to his lips. "Shh. No second-guessing. No regrets. We made a deal to simply take it as it comes, moment to moment. So let's just enjoy today. Please?"

"You're sure?"

She nodded.

He took a deep breath. "Okay." He cocked his head, a crooked smile curving his lips. "You own a pair of jeans?"

She shook her head, her hair as bright as the bars of sunlight striping the floor.

"Aw, come on. Not a single pair?"

"No." She thought for a moment. "But Charlie may have left some here that I could wear. I'll have to check in the utility room."

"Good. What about boots?"

"This is Montana," she said dryly. "They're required."

"Great." He put his arm around her slender shoulders and led her out of the kitchen and up the stairs. He stopped before the bathroom door, ignoring the urge to keep on going until they reached the bedroom, where clothing definitely wouldn't matter.

She looked up at him. "What do you have in mind?"

"A shower, first. And then—" He tucked a silky sheaf of soft blond hair behind her ear, leaned down and pressed an openmouthed kiss to the satiny hollow at the crook of her throat. "Then I'm going to teach you how to fly."

"I'm no expert, but I don't think these fit quite right."

Victoria walked down the porch steps. Feeling self conscious, she glanced down at the faded denim of Charlie's jeans. Her fingers plucked nervously at the fabric.

The jeans were tight, molded to her narrow waist and slim thighs like a second skin. A pair of buckskin cowboy boots added inches to her height, while a sleeveless, open-throated blue blouse echoed the color of her eyes and her thick straight hair fell like a pale gold curtain below her shoulders. She felt strange; as different on the outside as she felt on the inside. She glanced shyly at Dare, awaiting his reaction.

He leaned back against the Harley and crossed his arms. The negligent posture seriously strained the soft black cotton of his T-shirt and the almost-washed-white of his old jeans. A pair of aviator sunglasses hid his eyes, but it didn't matter as that slightly off-center smile that always stole her breath suddenly lit up his face. "I'd hate to see them if they were any righter, darlin'," he drawled. "As it is, they're playing hell with the fit of *my* jeans."

Pleasure bloomed inside her. Just as she had last night, she found herself thinking that even though he was going to leave in less than a week, she'd never regret this time and what was happening between them. She smiled.

"Come on." He straightened abruptly and held out his hand.

She eyed the bike warily. "Are you sure about this?"

"What's the matter? Don't you trust me?"

Her chin came up. "Of course I do." To prove it, she laid her palm in his, only to give a squeak of surprise as he tugged her against him.

"Good." He lowered his head to press a scorching kiss to her lips.

By the time they came up for air, she could barely stand. She was still trying to catch her breath when he strapped a helmet on her head and she found herself straddling six hundred pounds of gleaming metal, her boots propped on the passenger pegs, her arms locked tightly around his waist. A thrill of anticipation went through her as he turned the key and hit the starter button. The bike rumbled to life, settling into a steady purr like an oversize jungle cat.

Balancing the heavy machine between his thighs, Dare rocked it forward off the kickstand, then depressed the clutch, pressed the shift lever with his foot and fed the machine some gas. "Hold on," he called, opening up the throttle.

Victoria squeezed her eyes shut. For the space of a second, she was sixteen again, in possession of her first driv-

er's license. In her mind, she could hear Aunt Alice's stern
lecture about the responsibility inherent in operating a mo-
torized vehicle, of the hazards of fast cars and fast men,
of—

The rest of her aunt's discourse was drowned out by a
throaty roar as the sleek machine shot forward. She gave a
shriek of muffled laughter as the initial momentum knocked
her back. She held on to Dare for dear life. The wind
whipped the ends of her hair as the Harley shot out of the
driveway and down the street. To her surprise, she felt no
fear, only exhilaration as the bike knifed through the bright
summer air.

She gave herself up to the day. They took the old two-lane
highway that led north out of Gage. The road unwound like
a black satin ribbon. It was hemmed in by tall fences, but
the surrounding grazing land was empty, the cattle having
been moved to higher summer pasturage.

Mountains rose on both horizons. They were squat in the
east, with rounded tops, while to the west the advance line
of the Rockies soared, dominating the skyline like a cren-
ellated castle wall. Year-round snow topped them.

The air was crystal clear, sweet with the scent of warm
summer grass; yet fall was foreshadowed by the stands of
aspen and alder that were already beginning to turn silver
and gold.

Victoria held on to Dare, her thighs cradling his, her
breasts pressed to his back, her hands splayed against the
washboard hardness of his warm belly. He'd been wrong,
she decided. Riding tandem wasn't like flying, it was more
like slow dancing. He led and she followed, so swiftly at-
tuned to him that after a while they moved as one. The experience was decidedly erotic, all warmth and motion and
heightened sensation. Victoria savored it, filled with a spar-
kling sense of elation and a happiness so sharp it hurt.

They stopped for lunch at a crossroads that boasted a tiny
log cabin restaurant. The proprietor was a taciturn, bearded

man in flannel and cowboy boots, a baseball cap glued to his grizzled head. Moose and elk heads dotted the cabin walls; adorned with glass eyes, the stuffed beasts appeared to watch them as they ate. Victoria couldn't wait to escape, but Dare seemed oddly pleased, claiming that the place looked exactly the way Montana was supposed to.

It was early evening by the time they finally rolled into Victoria's driveway. Dare killed the Harley's engine and rocked the kickstand into place, but neither of them made a move to climb off the bike. Instead, they sat in companionable silence, soaking up the immense quiet.

"Tired?" Dare asked finally, twisting around to look at Victoria over his shoulder.

She pulled off the helmet and handed to him, wrapping her arms around his waist. She leaned her cheek against his broad, warm back, enjoying the way his muscles flexed as he hung the helmet on the handlebar by the chin strap.

She yawned. "Uh-huh. I think I could use a nap." She pressed a kiss to the cleft of his spine.

Beneath her ear, his heart speeded up. "Keep that up and the one thing you're *not* going to get is a nap," he said gruffly.

Her pulse skittered, but before she could tell him that was fine with her, Mrs. Vonnegut came bustling out on her porch. She waved frantically to get their attention. "Victoria, Mr. Kincaid! Help! Please! I'm afraid I've... I've set my kitchen on fire!" Her voice rose dramatically as she clutched her hands together and beseeched them to come to her aid.

"Oh, my word!" Responding automatically to the little old lady's cry of distress, Victoria clambered off the motorcycle. She started toward the gate, only to have Dare catch up with her before she'd gone more than a few feet.

"What do you think you're doing?" he growled, surging past her to block the way.

"What do you think? You know we can't stand by and do nothing while Doris's house burns down!"

"Hell." He turned and popped the newly installed latch loose. "I knew you were going to say that." He yanked open the gate. "Stay behind me," he ordered. He took a single step, only to jerk to a stop and murmur something rude under his breath.

Victoria ran right into his back, unable to see a thing except his broad shoulders. "What is it? What's the matter?"

"See for yourself," he muttered, reaching around and tugging her to his side.

Victoria blinked. "Oh, my."

Mrs. Vonnegut's backyard was dotted with cloth-covered tables, each one groaning under the weight of an assortment of casserole and salad dishes. Crepe paper festooned the trees and bushes, a beer keg was set up in the shade under the porch and a large white sheet cake with the message *Congratulations, Dare and Victoria* spelled out in green icing occupied a place of honor under an awning anchored to the side of the house.

Dumbstruck, Victoria looked around at a sea of smiling faces. At first glance, it appeared half the town had turned out.

"Surprise!" came a chorus of voices.

It appeared Mrs. Vonnegut was throwing them a belated wedding reception.

It was a typical Gage gathering. The partygoers were a conservative, traditional, hardworking group who were happy for a break in routine and the excuse to get together for a visit. While they ranged in age from infants to octogenarians, they quickly drifted into two groups, men in one, women in the other, a pattern that had existed for as long as anyone could remember.

The women talked about the yield on their gardens, the coming school year, their children and their men. The men discussed cattle prices, the weather, the likelihood that the governor would win another term in the upcoming election and the women.

The children ran back and forth between the two groups, not talking about anything in particular but grateful to have one last party before school started for the year.

The only thing that was different, Victoria thought, as the party progressed into its second hour and she slipped away from a knot of women to dip herself a glass of nonalcoholic punch, was *her*. For the first time in her life, she felt as if she fit in.

She had Dare and their bogus marriage to thank for that.

At first, as people had oohed and aahed over her changed appearance, kidded her about riding a "hog" and made approving comments about her landing herself a hero for a husband—Doris having spread the word about Dare's bravery in saving little Amy—she'd felt so guilty about the deception, she'd been tempted to confess everything.

But then, as she'd continued to talk to people, she'd begun to realize it wasn't the lie they were responding to—it was her. *She* was different. The time she'd spent with Dare had changed her. She wasn't afraid to be herself anymore, to show her true feelings rather than reflect everyone else's. After years of standing on the sidelines, watching the merry-go-round of life spin without her, she'd not only jumped on, she'd taken her courage in her hands and grabbed the gold ring. And wonder of wonders, while the earth *had* moved, the sky hadn't fallen or the ground opened to swallow her.

She wasn't so naive as to think there wasn't going to be a price to pay for what had happened to her. Change was never without cost, and the little voice in her head—the one that was always brutally honest—kept reminding her that come next week, after she testified, Dare was going to walk out of her life as quickly as he'd walked in.

It wasn't something she viewed lightly. Just the thought hurt; she wasn't sure how she was going to survive the reality. She loved him; it had taken her thirty years to find him. But they'd made a deal. And when she weighed the heartache to come against never having had the experience of knowing him at all, she couldn't regret what she'd done.

In much the same way, she also knew that there would be no going back to the way things had been before. And rather than alarm, she felt liberated. She wasn't sure what she was going to do, if she would leave Gage or stay, but she knew she was going to do something. She wasn't afraid anymore. The world suddenly held a host of possibilities that she wanted to explore.

"How're you doing?" Dare came up behind her and laid a big, warm hand on her shoulder.

She turned and raised her gaze to his, a warm feeling spiraling through her at the genuine concern in his voice. "I'm fine. How about you?"

He studied her for a moment, as if to make sure she was telling the truth. He shrugged. "I'm holding my own." He hesitated, then smiled unexpectedly, in that brief but breathtaking way he had. "Actually, I guess you could say I'm doing better than that. I've had several job offers. I think everyone's afraid you're going to get stuck supporting me."

Her eyes lit with amusement. "Fate worse than death for a Montana man," she observed dryly.

His smile deepened. "That seems to be the consensus. I've been trying to tell 'em I'm a modern guy, that it's okay by me if you want to take care of me, but they aren't buying it."

She clucked her tongue sympathetically. "That's right. No freeloaders allowed around here."

"Well then, I guess I'll have to let you make it up to me. You can start with a dance."

With a ripple of surprise, she looked around to find dusk had fallen and it was near dark. Several couples were already swaying across the lawn in time to the music blaring from the portable stereo set up on Doris's back porch.

Dare didn't have to ask her twice. She slid her hand into his. "I'd love to," she said sincerely, stepping into his arms. The song was a slow one; due to the disparity of their heights, it took them a few bars to figure out how to handle it, but they were soon moving together as if they'd been doing it for years.

A rowdy country song came next, with people joining in from the sidelines to form a loose line dance. Finding themselves in the middle of the crush, Victoria and Dare tried to follow along, much to the delight of a handful of her former students, who shouted encouragement. By the time the music changed again, everyone was flushed and out of breath.

Victoria went gratefully back into Dare's arms, her cheeks pink from laughing, sighing with pleasure as he pulled her close. They fell into a comfortable silence, rocking to the gentle beat of an old George Strait song.

"Victoria?" The song was half-over before Dare spoke.

"Hmm?" She rubbed her cheek against his shirtfront.

"Are you going to be okay when this is over?"

She leaned back so she could see him, her expression sobering at the troubled look on his face. "What's the matter?"

"You tried to tell me what my being your husband was going to do to your life, and I was too damn arrogant to listen. Now, seeing all this—" a helpless look crossed his face as he made a slight gesture with his chin that encompassed the party "—I think I'm finally starting to understand what I've done."

Tenderness spread through her like warm honey. "It really is all right. You did me a favor."

"Right." His skeptical tone made his opinion of that clear.

"You did." She tried to decide how best to explain, then realized the best thing she could do was tell the truth. "How much did Doris tell you about my aunt?"

He considered before he answered. "Not much. I gather she had a pretty strong opinion about things. And that you were devoted to her."

"How diplomatic." Victoria mouth curved in a half smile. "The truth is, for all that I loved her, she was a benevolent dictator. According to Aunt Alice, both my parents were headstrong and impetuous. She didn't want me to be the same way, so she was always cautioning me. After a while . . . I became the person she thought I should be. But deep down, there's always been this part of me that longed for a little adventure . . . Only I didn't want to risk anything to have it."

His gaze was thoughtful as he looked down into her face. "The cruise . . . ?"

She nodded. "Exactly. I guess in the back of my mind, I thought I'd just have a taste—like an appetizer, if you will. If it was too spicy, too strange and different, I could always set it aside and go back to my safe, secure, bland life. Except it didn't quite work out that way. I went looking for adventure and it followed me home. And the funny thing is, I'm glad. It made me see that nothing is as safe and secure as it seems. And that if you're not willing to take a risk, then the thing you want is probably not worth having." *Like you,* she thought, savoring the solid feel of him beneath her hands.

Something strong and complicated darkened his eyes. "Your aunt was lucky to have you," he said quietly.

She let him draw her closer. "I was lucky to have my aunt."

Dancing under the canopy of stars in the vast Montana sky, they finished the song in silence.

When the music finally ended, Victoria took a deep breath and sent Dare a shy smile. "Could we go home? Please?"

He broke the link of his hands around her waist and reached up to lightly stroke her chin with the ball of his thumb. "You sure you want to do that? People are going to talk."

"As far as I can tell, between the jeans and the motorcycle, I've blown my reputation as a lady. I might as well do something to make myself happy."

"*I* think you're a lady. Sometimes, anyway," he added with mock solemnity.

"Thank you—I think. So what do you say we sneak out of here?"

It wasn't as easy as that, of course. It took them several circuits of the party before they located Doris, who was in the kitchen chatting with several of her cronies. The elderly lady beamed at them as they said good-night, dismissing their thanks with an airy gesture. "It was the least I could do," she said, fondly patting Victoria's hand. "Particularly after what your young man did for my Amy. He's a real hero, my dear."

Victoria felt Dare tense at her side. Puzzled, she wondered at it, only to have her attention claimed as Mrs. Vonnegut leaned forward.

"Why don't you two go out through the front," the elderly lady suggested, her eyes twinkling. "That way you can avoid the comments you're sure to get, otherwise, about leaving early."

Quick to see the wisdom of the suggestion, they did just that. They were at the front door when Pam Craig caught up with them. "Miss Cooper?"

Victoria stopped and turned around. "Why, Pam...hello. I saw Charlie earlier, but I didn't know you were here, too."

"I had to work. I just got off a little while ago." Pam brushed a strand of dark blond hair behind her ear. Her gaze touched briefly on Dare who was holding the screen open for Victoria. She nodded at him before bringing her gaze back to Victoria. "Do you have a minute?"

"I'm afraid we were just leaving..."

"Please?"

Victoria wanted in the worst way to say no, but the younger woman's expression stopped her. She turned to Dare, intending to tell him to go ahead, but was forestalled as he said, "I'll wait for you outside," and went out on the porch to do just that.

"I won't keep you long," Pam said. "It's just... I was watching you and your husband a few minutes ago, and I wanted you to know, I've come to a decision. About... about Will and me."

A little confused by what possible connection there could be between her and Dare and the younger couple's relationship, Victoria said, "Oh."

"It's just..." Pam twisted a piece of long blond hair between her fingers. "I had decided to take Will back. I know... I know he hasn't been very nice to you, Miss Cooper," she said in a rush, "but sometimes, when it's only the two of us... he can be so sweet, not like he is with other people. And I really do love him, and I get so lonesome..."

The younger woman's anguish was unmistakable. Victoria's heart went out to her. "Oh, Pam—"

Charlie's sister raised her hand. "Please, just listen." She swallowed. "Like I said, I'd decided to take Will back, and then, when I got here tonight, I saw you out on the lawn, dancing with Mr. Kincaid. You look so... happy, Miss Cooper. I mean, when I first saw you, in those clothes—" she gestured at Victoria's boots and jeans "—with your hair down, I almost didn't recognize you. But it's more than that... When you look at Mr. Kincaid, you just seem to light up. And when he looks at you... well, that's how I want Will to look at me. Not just like he wants to get me into bed, but with respect, as if he'd die for me if he had to... As if I'm really special."

Victoria couldn't think what to say. Truth to tell, she was a little embarrassed by how transparent her own feelings must be if Pam could read them so easily. And troubled that the young woman had so misread Dare's, seeing something that just wasn't there.

Pam straightened her shoulders. "It made me realize that I can't expect Will to respect me if I don't respect myself. So I've decided to tell him that from here on in, Charlie and I are a package deal. And that either he can go to counseling and really work with me on our marriage—or we can call it quits."

"I—I don't know what to say," Victoria said. "But I hope it works out for you."

To Victoria's astonishment, Pam closed the distance between them and gave her a quick hug. "You don't have to say anything," she said softly. "I just wanted to tell you...thanks. For the way you've tried to help Charlie and me. And that I'm happy for you, that you found someone. You deserve it." And with that, Pam straightened and walked away, leaving Victoria bemused as she went out to join Dare.

"Everything okay?" he said, emerging out of the shadows at the bottom of the stairs.

"Yes," she answered, still sorting through what Pam had said as they crossed the lawn toward her house. "I think so. I think Pam just did some growing up."

"I take it that's good?"

"For Pam and Charlie? Yes. I don't think Will is going to like it, but then, I don't think he likes very much."

They were silent as they went up the stairs. Dare unlocked the back door and they stepped inside. "Stay here," he said firmly. As quiet as a ghost, he slipped away to check out the rest of the house.

In what seemed like mere seconds, he was back, materializing out of the darkness so suddenly, Victoria gave an involuntary gasp when he whispered, "All clear."

He slipped his arms around her, tipped her head back and kissed her. His mouth found hers unerringly in the dark.

She reached up and framed his face in her hands, kissing him back. He smelled of soap, fresh air and warm male, which on him was a potent aphrodisiac.

She sighed with pleasure when they finally came up for air, leaning against him since she wasn't sure her legs would hold her. "Dare?" She pressed closer, the ache at the core of her growing stronger at the feel of his arousal thrusting against her.

"What?" He turned his head, brushing her fingers with his mouth.

"This time, when we make love, can we leave on the light? I want to see you. I want to see . . . us."

There was a moment of stunned surprise, then a hoarse, rusty laugh sounded in her ear. "Aw, Teach. You really are full of surprises."

And then he took her up to bed and proceeded to teach her she wasn't the only one.

Ten

Stripped to the waist, Dare whistled tunelessly between his teeth as he scrubbed with a soapy rag at the Harley's fender.

The August day was quickly becoming a scorcher, without so much as the rumor of a breeze to stir the leaves. He could feel the sting of the sun's rays across his shoulder blades.

He glanced across the yard. Victoria sat in the gazebo. She had her lesson planner open in front of her, a stack of books at her elbow and a pencil in her hand, but to his surprise she wasn't working. Instead, she'd tipped her chair back and was sitting with her face lifted to the light-washed sky.

He wondered what had her so transfixed. Squinting against the glare, he followed her gaze until he saw the eagle soaring high overhead, swooping and gliding as it rode the heated air currents. Captured by the power and beauty of the big bird's flight, he watched until it disappeared from sight.

His gaze met Victoria's as he lowered his eyes. They exchanged a long look of shared appreciation for what they'd witnessed, before they both went back to work.

That effortless ability to communicate startled him.

It was almost as if they were really married.

Except they weren't, he reminded himself sharply, scraping off a splotch of tar stuck to the bike's chrome trim with his thumb. In three days, he'd be gone; there was only today and the weekend left and then, on Monday, probably in the early afternoon, a pair of marshals would arrive to escort Victoria to Billings for the trial. He would be free to go.

So? He began to wash the bike's front fender. That had been the plan all along. They had a deal. He'd told Victoria right up front, before they ever made love, he was leaving when the assignment was done. She knew the score.

The question was, did he? Did he even know what game he was playing? Hell. *Was* he playing?

It sure didn't feel like it. As much as he wanted to pretend otherwise, the thought of saying goodbye sent a chill through him that had nothing to do with the contrast between the heat beating down on his back and the water gushing out of the hose at his feet.

He tried to tell himself his concern was all for Victoria.

He knew she cared for him. He could see it in her eyes whenever she looked at him, hear it in her voice every time she said his name, feel it in her touch when they made love.

Despite her assurances to the contrary, he worried about what would happen to her when he was gone. What was she going to tell people? How was she going to explain? How would she get along without someone to look out for her? Heck, she'd probably starve to death. If she didn't poison herself first...

He sighed. He could make all the jokes he wanted, but he wasn't fooling himself. As much as he hated to admit it,

Victoria's future wasn't his only concern. For the first time since Jimmy had died, he was actually considering his own.

He'd never thought much about tomorrow. But when he had, he'd always expected to spend it alone. His father's desertion had taught him not to depend on anybody but himself. And his failure to make it up to his mother had taught him not to let anybody depend on him.

But this last week and a half with Victoria had been different, somehow. *She* was different. Soft when he expected tough, proud when he expected soft, vulnerable when he braced for sassy and intractable when he was foolhardy enough to think she'd yield.

He had to admit, the thought had crossed his mind that she'd be a challenge for a lifetime.

If a man was in the market for that sort of thing. Which he wasn't, he reminded himself. If his parents' example hadn't been enough, he'd had a front-row seat for the three-ring circus that Jimmy's marriage had become prior to his friend's death. There was nothing like watching a relationship self-destruct to put the whole love-and-marriage issue in proper perspective. Unless it was watching the result: the total disintegration of a man you really admired who also happened to be your best friend....

All of which was water under an old, old bridge, he reminded himself. And didn't help him deal with the strange, unwanted yearnings Victoria created in him.

The bottom line was, he didn't know how he felt.

And he only had a few days left to figure it out.

He picked up the hose. Blocking the end with his thumb to create a spray, he began to rinse the bike, only to frown as the water abruptly dwindled away. Automatically, he gave the hose a shake, then peered down at the end, only to give a yelp as it suddenly squirted out in an icy spray that drenched his face.

"Sonofagun!" He jerked it away from himself as if it were a snake, then twisted around as an indistinct sound came from behind him and he found the source of the problem.

Victoria stood with the hose clutched between her hands. Even without the still-visible kink in the rubber, her guilty smile was a dead giveaway that she was responsible for the water dripping down his face. "Gotcha."

Without a moment's hesitation, Dare slicked back his wet hair, clamped his thumb back over the end of the hose and turned the spray on her.

He had to give her credit. She gave a shriek as the cold water struck her, wetting the front of her dress, but she didn't lose her head. Instead, she quickly flexed the length of rubber in her hands and pinched off the water supply again.

"That wasn't very nice," she said, her voice filled with laughter.

"I've been accused of a lot of things in my life," he said, deadpan, "but 'nice' isn't one of them." To prove his point, he shifted his gaze from her face to the water-soaked fabric over her breasts. She had on the white dress she'd been wearing the day they'd met. At the moment, the damp fabric was almost transparent, revealing the pale crests of her nipples, peaked from the sudden cold.

As bold as a pirate, he stepped close and pressed the pad of his thumb to one pebbled circle. Their eyes met. Victoria shivered. And leaned forward, into his caress.

As fast as that, the need to brand her as his own poured through him.

Dare dropped his hand and caught one of hers, linking their fingers. "Come on," he said hoarsely. With a brief detour to turn off the water, he tugged her toward the house. As if sensing the strength of the desire riding him, Victoria didn't speak; anticipation hung in the air between them.

Once inside, he shut the door, snapped on the dead bolt and turned, trapping her against the smooth wood. They came together in a fusion of heat, an explosion of mutual need melding them together as his mouth came down on hers.

This kiss was no chaste preamble, no gentle prelude to a greater ardor. It was instantly carnal.

Victoria clung to him. With every shuddery breath, the already erect tips of her breasts rubbed against him through the damp material of her dress. He lifted his head, staring into the delicate planes of her face. Her head was thrown back, her eyes closed, her thick dark-gold lashes feathered against her baby-fine skin. Her lips were rosy, slicked from his mouth; they trembled as she sighed and opened her eyes, staring up at him out of twin slices of blue brighter than the sky outside.

He still couldn't believe the depth of her passion, the un-restrained way she gave herself up to him, the swift and complete transformation that overcame her as she let go and met his desire with her own.

It was exciting. Overwhelming. And humbling, infusing the need surging through him with an overlay of tender-ness.

It was that tenderness that gave him the strength to en-sure their privacy. Leaving her leaning against the door, he made a quick circuit of the room, wrenched down the shades, blocking out the bright sunlight pouring through the windows until the room glowed with a pale amber light like the inside of an imperial topaz.

"You remember the morning I cut my hand?" The dif-fuse light painted Victoria in gold as he took her hand, led her across to the countertop and lifted her onto it.

"Yes." Her eyes locked on his as he stepped into the vee of her thighs. She clasped her hands around his neck.

He didn't miss the way her eyes darkened as she recalled what *hadn't* transpired between them. There was so little he could give her, but he could take the remembered sting of that day away, he thought fiercely. "I wanted you. So much I hurt. And later...later, when I thought about it, I'd picture what I wanted to do. It always started like this..."

His head dipped then and his lips drifted across hers as light as a feather. His teeth raked gently over her bottom lip, then his tongue stroked the seam of her lips until she parted them. He plumbed the depths of her mouth, the motion slow, unhurried, evocative, as his tongue slid in and out. His hands skated down, his fingers trailing over the side swell of her breasts before closing around her narrow waist. He drew her close, rotated his hips, let her feel the effect she had on him.

Pressed together, mouth to mouth, lower bodies fused, they kissed, tongues tangled, purposefully going slow as they rocked together in an unhurried preview of the pleasure to come. The cost of Dare's restraint grew quickly evident in the rigid configuration of his muscles, the tension that slabbed his chest and belly, his arms, shoulders and thighs. It was obvious in the perspiration that dampened the ebony hair at the nape of his neck, that slicked his back and trickled down his spine.

Gasping, Victoria let loose of him to lean back and brace herself on hands that shook. "Dare..."

"I'm right here," he rasped, opening his mouth over the pulse throbbing in her throat. Careful not to bruise her delicate skin, he stroked it with the tip of his tongue. Heat grew inside him, shimmering to match the hushed golden air. He explored the fragile line of her jaw, the silky warmth where her collarbones met, the glossy skin above the modest scoop neck of her dress.

Eventually, he lifted his head. "Victoria?" His fingers closed on the garment's top button. He willed her to open her eyes.

Not until she did, not until her lashes fluttered up and she focused on him, her eyes a slumberous, sky-washed blue, did he slide the button free and, as he'd once fantasized, push back the fabric to expose the globes of her breasts. He paused, the breath locking in his throat as he discovered she wasn't wearing a bra, and then he cupped her warm, trembling flesh in his hands. A quick glance revealed a flush of arousal pinking her cheeks. He rolled the sensitive points of her nipples between his fingers. "So pretty." He lowered his head, pressed a kiss to each crest, before he settled his mouth over one thrusting tip, savoring her indrawn breath at the intimate caress.

He forced himself to go slow, to savor each moment. He drew on her with his lips, shaped her with his tongue, nipped gently with his teeth. He didn't stop until she was bowed in his arms, her neck arched back, her hair sliding like silk over his bare arm.

And then, just as he'd once imagined, he tossed her skirt out of his way and ran his hands up the inside of her thighs.

Only this time, he didn't stop there. This time, he freed himself from his jeans, yanked the lace scrap of Victoria's panties out of his way and filled her with himself. Both of them cried out at the first long slide of connection.

Victoria locked her legs around his back. He wrapped his arms around her waist and pulled her closer. The harsh tangle of their breathing was the only sound in the hushed, sun-filled room. That, and the slick, damp sound they made as they came together, hard to soft, the small of his back hollowing as he thrust, his movement measured as she clung to his broad shoulders.

He set a slow, deliberate pace. There was something dreamlike about the hazy golden light, the stillness of the

hot summer afternoon, the suppressed power as they met
and drew apart. Slowly, slowly, they melted together, two
separate beings becoming one, same heartbeat, same respi-
ration, same wildness throbbing in their blood, same ach-
ing need trembling on the edge of fulfillment.

Victoria's breath came in labored gasps. "Dare—" She
cried his name, her fingernails pricking his shoulders as the
first flare of fulfillment caught her unprepared. "Oh, Dare.
I—" She gasped and gave herself up as a cannonade of
pleasure burst inside her.

I love you. The words whispered through Dare. He re-
coiled with shock, telling himself they were an echo of hers,
not a declaration of his own, that he'd merely finished her
sentence. And then her climax triggered his own and he
couldn't think, he could only feel, the sensation so acute, it
was as if he were being pulled inside out, as if there were no
more her or him, only an...us.

When it was done, they clung together, holding each other
up. Dare felt wiped out, drained, complete; he couldn't find
it in himself to regret what they'd just shared.

Yet, a tide of uneasiness lapped at the shores of his satisfaction as his reason returned and three little words sliced
through him.

I love you... It wasn't true, of course. The thought had
been nothing more than an outgrowth of the moment, an
overflow of sexual tension. To prove it, he opened his eyes
to look at the woman in his arms, only to be struck by the
utter serenity on her face, the total trust with which she
leaned against him.

All of a sudden, it hurt to breathe. Something immense
swelled in his chest, clawed at his throat, something so intense, it struck at the very heart of him—

A faint thump came from the front of the house. Victoria's lashes fluttered up. "Relax," she said huskily, mis-
reading the strain in his face. "It's just Fred with the mail."

His heart pounding uncomfortably, Dare averted his face and fixed his eyes on the oven clock. "He's late."

She gave a languid sigh and buried her face against his damp throat. "It's probably the heat. It slows everybody down. Heaven knows, I feel as if I could melt. How about a shower?"

"Sure."

She stroked her tongue against his hot skin.

Desire ignited inside him, wiping away his satiation. A chill feathered over him as he realized he wanted to lift her into his arms, carry her up to bed and make love to her again. That he was damn close to being totally out of control.

He shifted away, yanked up his jeans and lifted her down from the counter. His hands trembled as he zipped his jeans; chagrined, he stuck them into his back pockets. "You go ahead."

"But..."

"I'll be right there. I want to take a look at the mail."

She looked at him uncertainly, searching his face, but didn't protest. "Okay," she said softly. "I'll see you in a few minutes."

Dare never came upstairs.

On some level, she'd expected it, Victoria realized, as the water turned cold and she finally gave up waiting for him and climbed out of the shower.

There'd been a certain tension crowding him after they made love, an inner turbulence that had been impossible to miss. Aware of her lack of experience with men, she'd assumed he merely needed a moment alone.

Now, she wasn't so sure. Shivering in the warm air, foreboding settled over her like a fog. She toweled dry, struck with a sudden sense of urgency, combed the tangles out of her hair and dressed. Barefoot, she hurried down the stairs.

Dare was in the kitchen, on the phone. She could hear the anger in his voice and his effort to control it before she ever crossed the threshold.

"I don't care if he's been abducted by aliens with ten feet and two heads!"

His gaze flicked over her as she walked in, taking in her damp hair and bare feet. Then, without so much as a nod of acknowledgment, he turned his back.

Victoria felt as if she'd been slapped. Cautioning herself not to overreact, she tried to figure out what could have happened to cause such a change in his manner.

Dare resumed his conversation. "No, you listen, lady. You find McDunna and have him call me. I don't care where he is. You tell him there's been a development in the Cooper case, and have him call me at the number I gave you. You got it?"

There was a loud squawk, presumably of protest on the other end of the line, which he dealt with by saying, "Just do it!" before he hung up with barely restrained violence.

Victoria gave him a moment, then took a deep breath. "Dare?"

The long muscles bracketing his spine tightened. He turned and gave her a long look that was frightening for its blankness. She might have been a total stranger, so cool and impersonal was his gaze. There was none of the warm appreciation she'd grown accustomed to the past few days or the proprietary air she hadn't even known was there until now, when it was missing.

"What?" Even his voice sounded different. Brusque and impatient.

"What is it? What's wrong?"

A nerve twitched in his jaw. He pointed to the table behind her. "See for yourself."

Twisting, all she saw at first was the usual stack of her mail, including a pair of periodicals, some brightly colored advertising fliers and several bills. Then she noticed the rectangle of cheap card stock off to one side. She stared at it, puzzled, until she registered the subdued blue border, the careful block printing and the small gold seal still attached to one end.

"You got another threat." His voice was carefully devoid of emotion. "It was in with today's mail."

She stepped closer to the table. Careful not to touch the note, she leaned down until she could read the message.

It was almost identical to the first one.

I WARNED YOU. I WON'T AGAIN. BACK OFF—OR ELSE.

A sick feeling cramped her stomach. She frowned as she realized it was more a reaction to Dare's agitation than it was to the threat itself. While it bothered her that someone continued to want to intimidate her, she didn't see how this second threat changed anything. As a matter of fact, there was actually some small comfort in the discovery it was essentially the same as the last. Whoever had sent it was clearly not too inventive, which was reassuring, under the circumstances. If somebody was out to get her, she'd prefer that they not be particularly clever.

She didn't think she'd point that out to Dare, however. Not when she recalled his reaction to her comments about the first threat. "So." She looked up from the note. "I take it Mr. McDunna was out?"

He stared at her. "You get a threat and that's it?" His voice rose. "You want to know about McDunna?"

She bristled a little at his tone. "Look, I realize it's unfortunate but—"

"Unfortunate!"

She raised her chin. "But at least, this time, I'm not alone. This time, you're here. Since I know you'll do whatever's best, I'm not sure what the problem is."

"The problem—" he said stiffly "—is pretty damn obvious. This is my fault."

It was her turn to stare. "I don't see how it can be," she said finally. "Not unless you wrote the thing yourself, which we both know isn't like—"

He cut her off. "There's no postmark."

It took a moment for the significance of what he was saying to sink in. "You mean—"

"I mean the bastard walked right up to the house and dropped it in your mailbox. If I'd just been doing my damn job instead of—"

"Don't." She couldn't stop her cry of protest. She wasn't sure what he was going to say but she knew she couldn't bear it if he reduced what had happened between them to something cheap and tawdry.

She struggled for composure. "For heaven's sake, Dare. Be reasonable. Whoever wrote this wouldn't have delivered it themselves if they thought they might get caught. For all we know, it may have been left while we were out in the backyard earlier. Or last night, for that matter. The sound we heard was probably exactly what we thought it was— Fred dropping off today's mail. Besides, it's not your job to apprehend the culprit. It's your job to protect me—which is what you've been doing."

"Oh, yeah. I'm doing a hell of a job of that," he said sarcastically.

"Yes, you are. Thanks to you, this old house is ten times more secure than it's ever been before. I haven't taken a step without you since you got here—and we both know it hasn't been because I haven't tried a few times. You've screened my calls, my friends, the mail." She paused for breath, saw he wasn't convinced and plunged on. "You were ready to sacrifice yourself for me during that incident with the lawn mower. You stood up for me even when it wasn't your fight, at the grocery store. And then there's the way you saved Amy—"

His expression turned even more frigid. "Anybody would've done the same thing."

"Anybody didn't. *I* didn't. The child's own mother didn't. For heaven's sake. Give yourself some credit. Even the Marshals Service recognizes how good you are at your job. They want you to teach about it. They even commended you for bravery."

The minute she said the last, she knew she'd struck a nerve. He went very still. "How do you know about that?"

"It was in the newspaper."

"Oh, really?" He was silent a moment, as if debating something with himself. Then his eyes hardened, and he said deliberately, "Well, let me tell you a few things that weren't. I'll bet a month's pay there was no mention that my partner's marriage was going all to hell, was there? Or that I suspected he was sneaking an occasional drink, but didn't report it? Or that his wife had called that day, right before we were due to leave for the courthouse and told him she'd filed for divorce? That I knew he ought to be relieved of duty, but let him talk me out of it? Is any of that in there?"

Prowling the room like a caged tiger, he answered his own question. "Hell, no! The truth is, I didn't do what I should have. And I walked away with a creased scalp, a flesh wound in my thigh, a five-dollar citation to hang on my wall—and Jimmy died." He gaze drilled into her, pinning her in place. "I let our friendship get in the way of my professional judgment, Victoria, and *I got him killed.* So don't tell me what a hero I am, okay?"

He expected her to be shocked, she realized.

And, in a way, she was. She was shocked that he couldn't see what he was doing to himself, that he was blaming himself for something that wasn't his fault. She was shocked at the burden he was carrying around, and that he believed a spate of self-condemning words would change her opinion of him.

She was shocked by how much she loved him. Not in spite of what he'd done—but because of it, since it had helped shape the man he was.

It was that love that gave her the courage to look him directly in the eyes and ask steadily, "What about Jimmy? What was *he* responsible for, Dare?"

He jerked as if she'd struck him. "What do you mean?"

"Exactly what I said. Didn't he have a responsibility? One to do the best he could? And, barring that, not to endanger you or your witness? Where's his blame?"

"For God's sake, Victoria. He's dead!"

"So you can forgive him—just not yourself?" She took a deep breath. "What if the situation had been reversed? Would you want him to blame himself if you'd been the one killed that day?"

"Forget it. Obviously, you don't understand—"

"I understand that you hold yourself responsible, although I don't agree with your reasoning. And I understand that you're trying to erect a wall between us."

His eyes darkened to the color of a storm sky. "Spare me the pop psychology," he said coldly. "The bottom line is, I've got no damn business letting my personal life get in the way of my job—which is to keep you safe. I let myself get sucked in for a while, let my sex drive do my thinking instead of my head, but that's over. From here on in, until the trial, we're back to being witness and marshal."

Even though she'd known it was coming, it hurt. She'd agreed to end things, yes, but not like...this. She forced herself to think, to ignore the hurt and the panic welling up inside her and concentrate. Why, she wondered with an edge of desperation, was he distancing himself from her now?

She had no hold on him. He'd made her no promises. She hadn't asked for any.

It didn't make any sense. Unless...

Unless it wasn't her he was trying to escape, but himself.

She turned the idea over in her mind, her heart thumping painfully as she tried to decide if it had actual merit or was merely the result of her own need to see this as something more than a casual fling.

She didn't think so. Not when she considered his refusal to acknowledge Jimmy's hand in what had happened to the other man. And not when she thought about the little boy he'd been. And not when she remembered the near desperation she'd sensed after they'd made love earlier.

She made one last attempt to reason with him. "If that's what you want, all right. But at least be honest. Why are you being so hard on yourself? What are you really afraid of, Dare?"

Something flickered in his gray eyes, something hot and dangerous like heat lightning, but his voice was flat and uncompromising. "Getting you killed."

"If your sole concern is my safety, there are other ways to guarantee it. We could lock ourselves in the house. Or go somewhere and check into a motel for the weekend. Either would be more effective than what you're proposing—"

"We had a deal," he interrupted coldly. "Nothing more than the moment—and the moment's *past.*"

Before she could respond, the phone shrilled.

Obviously glad for the interruption, he was across the room in two strides. He snatched up the handset as if it were a lifeline. "Kincaid," he barked. There was a pause and then he said in obvious surprise, "Mike? No, I just didn't expect it to be you. I'm waiting for McDunna and—"

Victoria watched as his expression smoothed out. Now that she knew what she was looking for, it was easy to see him set his emotions aside and assume that detached, impersonal air he used like a shield.

"*What?* He did? Just like that?"

Something in his voice—as if he'd gotten an unexpected shock—made her go very still.

"You're sure he's got it covered? Yeah? Well, okay. Yeah, I guess. I've always wanted to see Aruba. No, it shouldn't be any trouble. You know me. I travel light. No baggage— that's my motto."

His attempt to sound lighthearted was as phony as a two-headed penny. Victoria could hear the undercurrent of grimness in his voice.

"All right. Sure. Talk to you then."

He hung up, his movements slow and deliberate, and turned to face her. For just a moment, he had the oddest expression on his face, a combination of regret and relief, before he again grew detached. "That was Mike Arizzo, my boss. Raymond Jeffries died this morning."

Surprise splintered through her as he named the man she was due to testify against. "What?"

"He had a heart attack about 4:00 a.m. He'd been complaining about chest pain and they were in the process of transferring him from jail to the hospital when it hit. Even with the paramedics right there, he never had a chance."

She tried to take in what he was saying but it was so unexpected, the implications refused to sink in. She looked at him blankly. "But . . . what does it mean?"

"It means no trial. It means you don't have to testify. McDunna will issue a notice to the press for the evening papers and the TV news broadcasts. Once we're sure that all of Jeffries's friends have gotten the word, the danger to you will be over. Your life will be back to normal."

"But...what about you?"

"Me?" He gave a hollow laugh. "Don't you get it, Victoria? I've been reassigned. Come tomorrow, and I'm out of here."

Eleven

Eleven

The next day dawned cool and cloudy.

Victoria sat at the kitchen table, sipping tea while she pretended to read the newspaper. The midmorning light was silvery, the room filled with shadows. The threat of rain hung in the air, carried on a mild breeze that fluttered the leaves on the trees. The rise and fall of a lawn mower motor buzzed in the background; Charlie had arrived a half hour earlier to take on his weekly chore.

She yawned. She'd spent a miserable night. Unable to sleep, she'd replayed the previous day's events until her head ached from thinking. By dawn she'd concluded that she didn't regret what she'd said to Dare, only that she'd been unable to make him see what he was doing to himself. If only they'd had more time—

"Hey, Miss Cooper." Charlie let the screen slap behind him as he walked in. "The mower's out of gas. Can I get a few dollars so I can make a run to the service station and fill up the gas can?''

Jarred from her thoughts, it took Victoria a moment to get her bearings. When she did, she came to her feet. "Sure. Hang on a minute.''

The boy came farther into the room as she got her purse and carried it back to the table. She pulled a five-dollar bill out of her billfold and handed it to him.

"Thanks.''

"No problem. You know, there's no great rush, Charlie. I could run you over later in the car this afternoon. Or you could wait and we could do it tomorrow.'' She'd have time to spare when Dare was gone.

"Naw, that's all right.'' He studied her. "Are you all right? You look kind of tired.''

"I'm fine.'' She replaced her billfold, surprised to find he was still frowning when she glanced up. She dredged up a smile. "Really, I am. What's the matter?''

"Is Will giving you a hard time because of me?'' he asked suspiciously.

Victoria was taken aback by the question. "Not at the moment. Why do you ask?''

Watching her carefully, the teenager gestured toward the tabletop. "I just wondered why else he'd write you.''

Confused, Victoria looked down—and found herself staring at the threatening note that had materialized the previous day. The item lay facedown, precisely where it had been left at the end of her and Dare's conversation. The block printing of her name was clearly visible.

"Why—'' All the moisture had deserted her mouth and her voice came out a squeak. She swallowed. "Why do you think that's from Will?''

Charlie could barely contain his impatience. "Because. I recognize his writing.''

Victoria's knees buckled. She sank down, nearly missing the edge of the chair. "Are you certain?"

"Of course. He always puts those little curls on the C in Craig—just like it is there in Cooper. And he prints everything else because nobody can read his real writing. Besides, I was with Pam when she bought those card things for him in Bozeman. They were the only ones she could find that didn't have hearts and flowers and stuff on them. He sends them to her all the time. Every time they have a fight."

"Oh." It was an effort, but Victoria managed to say nothing more. Her thoughts churning, she realized she needed time to think about this before she said or did anything.

Charlie gave her a curious look. "So what's he want?"

Her mind went blank. "It's—it's an apology," she said finally, saying the first thing to come to mind.

The boy's eyebrows rose. "Really?" He shook his head. "I never would've guessed that." He shrugged, dismissing the vagaries of adults. "Well, I'd better get going. I want to get done before it rains." Pocketing the money she'd given him, he strolled out the door.

Victoria stared blankly after him, then slowly switched her gaze to the note.

Will. She had a sudden desire to laugh. All this time she'd been imagining a bogeyman in the bushes who wasn't there. It had never crossed her mind that the note writer was someone she knew. Here she'd been pining for a little excitement in her life, convinced she had to leave Gage to find it, and it had been right under her nose the whole time.

The irony didn't escape her. In a certain convoluted sense, she had Will to thank for Dare.

She stood to pour herself another cup of tea, trying to put her thoughts in some semblance of order so she could decide what to do.

She wasn't afraid of Will. He was a blowhard and a bully, but he wasn't a violent one; if he wanted to hurt her, he'd had plenty of opportunities these past few months and had chosen not to take them. Nor did she want to cause any more trouble for Pam and Charlie, or further disrupt their lives. Although Will obviously didn't believe it, she'd encouraged Pam to seek counseling in the hope it would help the couple's marriage. Having Will thrown in jail would put an end to any chance of that.

Still. That didn't negate the seriousness of what he'd done. Or mean that he should be allowed to get away with it, either. He needed to know, in no uncertain terms, that threatening people was a serious offense. A federal offense, to be precise, since he'd been dumb enough to actually mail that first note. There had to be a consequence for his action.

That brought her to the question of Dare.

She stood at the window, staring unseeingly out at the dismal day, and took a shallow sip of steaming tea. If she told him, she didn't doubt he'd take care of it—even though it wasn't technically his "duty." Chances were, due to the weekend, it would take a day or two to get all the loose ends nailed down.

The proper authorities would have to be notified, statements taken, evidence gathered before an arrest could be made. It was time she and Dare could conceivably spend together since the urgency of his need to protect her would be over. He would no longer have his job as an excuse to keep her at arm's length.

The thought of having even one more day with him made her ache with longing.

Yet even as she turned the idea over in her mind, she knew she wasn't going to tell him about Will. She'd spent too many years trying to be something she wasn't to expect the same thing from Dare. If there was one thing the past ten days had taught her, it was that the courage to change came from the inside out, not the other way around. She couldn't make him see what he chose not to. She couldn't make him love her. She couldn't change him.

She could only change herself.

She wasn't about to be like Aunt Alice, to make the same mistake her aunt had, no matter how well-meaning. She loved Dare enough to let him be who he was—even if that meant letting him go.

"Good morning."

Startled, she jerked around, sloshing hot tea on herself. With a muffled cry, she dropped the mug onto the counter and pressed her stinging hand to her mouth, her eyes on Dare, who stood poised in the hall doorway.

"You better run some cold water on that." He crossed the room and reached past her to turn on the tap, then stepped back, careful not to touch her.

His restraint wasn't lost on Victoria. She had to swallow around the lump that rose to her throat. "Thanks." She thrust her hand under the water.

He nodded. He was dressed much as he had been the first time she'd seen him, in jeans and a white shirt open at the throat, the sleeves rolled back to expose his forearms. He held a brown leather jacket in his hand.

His saddlebags were draped over his shoulder.

The pain of her scalded skin was minor when compared to the ache in her heart. She turned the water off and reached for a dish towel to dry her hands. "You about ready?"

"Looks like it. I just need to get that." He nodded at the note.

"But…why?" Now that she'd made the decision to deal with Will herself, the prospect of Dare finding out the truth was alarming.

"It's part of an ongoing investigation. I doubt they'll ever catch the person who sent it, but I still need to drop it off in Billings. They'll want to check it for fingerprints and add it to the case file."

"Oh." She realized she had no choice but to let him take it. She didn't think he'd believe her if she suddenly claimed to want the thing for a souvenir.

Dare laid his saddlebags out on the table. "You have one of those sealable plastic bags I can put it in?" he asked.

"Yes." She tugged her pale pink sweater down over her jeans and padded over to the pantry. Her bare feet didn't make a sound on the cool linoleum floor as she retrieved a small plastic bag from a roll on the shelf and handed it to him.

Their hands touched. Like a trip wire, the contact set off a slide of feelings inside her. Had it only been yesterday that he'd pressed her up against the door and kissed her? That he'd put his arms around her and joined his body to hers?

She almost cried out at the renewed sense of loss as he withdrew his hand. Pressing her lips together, she watched as he took a pencil, inserted it into the crease of the note, picked it up and slid it into the plastic sleeve. It only took him a second to lay it on top of his folded shirts and close the flap on the bag. "Well, I guess that's it."

He buckled the strap, shrugged into his jacket and slung the fine leather bags back over his shoulder. If he'd had a hat, he would've looked exactly like a gunslinger from the Wild West.

"Dare—"

He pulled his collar free. "What?"

"I—" She bit her lip and reminded herself she meant to let him go with her chin up and her dignity intact. "Nothing."

Their eyes met. He stared at her for a full, searching second. And then, without a word, he cupped her chin in his fingers, leaned forward and kissed her.

Their lips met and clung for a long breathless moment; Victoria poured all the love she felt for him into it, holding nothing back. She clenched her hands into fists, afraid if she reached for him, she wouldn't let go.

It was over too soon. He lifted his head. His hand fell away and he stepped back. "You take care."

She forced down the swell of emotion threatening to overwhelm her and took a step back of her own. "You, too."

He nodded, walked to the door and opened it. Before he could stop it, the little orange cat slipped inside. With a soft meow, the animal brushed up against his legs.

Dare looked uncertainly at Victoria.

"Don't worry," she said softly. "I'll take care of it."

He nodded. "Thanks." His gaze searched her face. He hesitated, his hand on the screen handle. "You sure you're going to be all right?"

"I'm going to be fine."

"If you need anything..." He had to stop to clear his throat. "Well, if you do, the marshals office in Billings can get word to me."

"Don't worry. Nothing is going to happen that I can't handle." She squared her shoulders. "Goodbye, Dare."

"See you, Teach." The screen opened and shut with a twang.

The cat meowed, more insistently this time. Victoria reached down, gathered it up and cuddled it against her. She stroked a hand over its bony little back. The animal began to purr despite the hot, salty tears suddenly splashing its soft fur.

Victoria watched as Dare strode across the porch and down the stairs.

He didn't look back.

* * *

He shouldn't have kissed her, Dare thought, gunning the Harley as he turned off of Victoria's road onto Gage's main street.

It had been a stupid, impulsive thing to do and now he was paying the price. He wanted her. Still. Which was saying a lot after all that stuff she'd thrown at him yesterday.

Not that he had any intention of giving in to such an unacceptable desire. It was for the best that their association had ended when it had. The way it had. After all, what was he going to do? Give up tracking fugitives full-time to become a P.O.D. again? Quit altogether and give up his gun for a suit? Buy a little house in the suburbs and settle down?

No way, he told himself, slowing to turn into the service station. One quick stop to fill up the bike and he was out of here.

He could hardly wait. He was anxious to get on the road, to put some miles between himself and this boring little town and get back to civilization. It was time to do some real work, to become some unsuspecting fugitive's worst nightmare.

He rolled to a stop by the pump. He shut off the engine, yanked off his helmet and hooked it over the handlebars. He climbed off and stretched his legs, then unscrewed the gas cap and inserted the hose nozzle, drumming the fingers of his free hand against the bike's gleaming black paint.

"Hey, Dare!" No more than a minute had passed when Charlie's voice snagged his attention.

He looked up to see the kid emerge from the station's interior. With a sense of disbelief, he realized he was actually glad to see the boy. And that knowing he wouldn't see Charlie again brought him no joy, but a sharp sense of loss. He frowned. He was definitely losing it. "Hey, Charlie. What's up?"

"I came to get some gas for the mower." The boy gestured to the other pump, where a dented container can sat

next to a beat-up old ten-speed with a basket on the back.
"What about you?" He took in Dare's coat and sunglasses, his eyes bright with curiosity as they came to rest on
the saddlebags attached to the back of the bike. "You going somewhere?"

Dare hesitated, uncertain what to say since he wasn't sure
what Victoria intended to tell people. "Yeah, I am. I've got
to take care of some out-of-town business. Keep on eye on
Victoria for me, okay?"

Charlie's gaze sharpened. He studied Dare's face, then
cocked his head. "You guys have a fight, or something?"

The kid was too damn smart for his own good. "Or
something." Dare kept his voice casual. "How's it going
with you?"

Charlie shrugged. "Okay, I guess. My sister got a new
job. Mrs. Perry hired her to work as a checker at the grocery store. That'll be good. More money, and she'll be home
nights."

"That's great," Dare said sincerely. The automatic shut-
off valve on the gas line tripped; he topped off the Harley's
tank, rehung the nozzle and replaced the gas cap. He
reached automatically for his wallet, then remembered it was
in his saddlebags, a preventive measure he'd taken ever since
he'd had one work its way out of his pocket a few years ago.
Replacing his credit cards and ID had been the pits.

He folded back the flap on the nearest bag and slid his
hand down inside, feeling for the distinctive square of
leather. "So what's your brother-in-law think of that?"

Charlie shrugged. "I don't know. He called this morning
and was coming by, so I imagine he and Pam are talking
about it now. That's all they do—talk. Yesterday morning,
they had a big fight and Pam told him to take a hike. Per-
manently. It was great. He went ballistic—but he went. Now
today he's back." The teenager shook his head, sending a
wedge of blond hair sliding across his forehead. "I'm never

getting married. All this love stuff—it's too complicated for me.''

Amen. Dare's fingers closed on his wallet. A gust of wind blew up, ruffling his shirt and hair. Before he could intercept it, the breeze picked up the note he'd laid on top of his things and sent it fluttering to land at Charlie's feet.

The boy retrieved it. He started to hand it to Dare, only to hesitate as he glanced at the rectangle of paper inside the plastic bag. Puzzlement, uncertainty and a flash of wariness all cartwheeled across his face. ''Don't tell me Will wrote you an apology, too?''

Dare started to pluck the item from the boy's fingers, then froze. ''What?''

''Well, that's what Miss Cooper claimed hers was.''

''Her what?''

''Her note from Will. It was there on the table. Back at the house. I asked her about it.'' Charlie's eyebrows knit. ''She acted as if were some great mental feat that I knew it was his handwriting. I told her how he's always writing stuff to Pam.''

Dare stared at the boy for one long moment. *Dammit.* Of course. It was so obvious he couldn't believe he'd missed it. Because of the timing of that first note, he and everyone else—Victoria, McDunna, the Marshals Service and the various agencies involved in the investigation—had concluded the threat had to do with the incident in Billings.

Instead, it had been nothing more than a coincidence.

Will's words to Victoria that day in the grocery store played through his head. *What's it take to get you to back off? Don't you pay attention? I warned you.*

Holy Saint Sophia. The guy couldn't have been more obvious if he'd worn a neon sandwich board that said Arrest Me.

And Dare had missed it. It had been right there, as plain as the nose on his face and he'd never given it a second thought. How the hell could he have overlooked something so glaring? He should've seen it. And he would have, if he'd been paying better attention, if he hadn't let his libido hijack his brain—

"It wasn't an apology, was it?" Charlie said, interrupting Dare's thoughts. "He wrote her something really awful, didn't he?" The boy's voice was thick with a combination of anger, humiliation and shame. "God! I'm so stupid! I should've known! I should've done something to stop him—"

"Hey—hold on!" Dare interjected, taken aback by the kid's distress. "Lighten up. This isn't your fault. You're not responsible for what Will does. He's the grown-up."

For some reason, the words sounded disturbingly familiar. He hesitated, forehead furrowed, and then yesterday's argument with Victoria came rushing back.

What about Jimmy? he heard her ask. *He was a grown man. Didn't he have a responsibility? Why are you being so hard on yourself?*

Dare gazed into Charlie's angry, anguished face and thought about what he'd just said. Suddenly, all those questions Victoria had asked took on a whole new meaning.

As did the answers.

Jimmy *had* had a responsibility, Dare acknowledged slowly. His friend had been a damn good marshal, but he'd been wrong not to take himself off the case. He'd been wrong to expect Dare to cover for him, wrong not to acknowledge he was going through a rough time and was a danger to himself, his friend and the witness he was sworn to protect.

Yet Dare hadn't wanted to see any of that. He'd been determined to defend his friend—even in death. In a pattern learned early on, Dare had shouldered the blame because it was better than acknowledging his anger.

Anger at Jimmy—for getting himself killed, for leaving Dare alone again.

Anger that had its source in his childhood, left over for the father who'd deserted him and the mother who'd left him to fend for himself as no adult should leave a child. But because she'd been all he'd had, Dare had loved and protected his mom as best he could, with all a child's unquestioning loyalty. And instead of blaming her for her shortcomings, he'd blamed himself.

He considered what had happened yesterday, remembering the moment when he'd put a name to his feeling for Victoria.

I love you. It was no longer a whisper, but a shout.

And what had he done? He'd panicked.

Everyone he'd ever loved had left him—father, mother, Jimmy. So when the new threat had come, and he'd had to face the fact that the danger he'd been downplaying was not just real, but close, he'd shut down, unable to face what it would mean if he lost Victoria, too. He winced as he recalled what he'd said to her.

We had a deal. Nothing more than the moment—and the moment's past.

And what had she done?

She'd taken responsibility for herself. She'd honored their "deal." She hadn't begged him to stay or blamed him for what had happened. She hadn't spoken a word of recrimination.

Because real love came without conditions.

His gaze cleared, his focus back on Charlie's distraught face. "Listen," he said firmly. "This is not your fault, trust me. Will's accountable for what he does. Not you. You just be the best kid you can, which is hard enough, and let the adults worry about the adult stuff. Okay?"

"But—"

"We'll talk about it some more. Later," Dare promised, yanking a ten-dollar bill from his wallet as raindrops began to paint the concrete with polka dots. "For now, put your bike and that can somewhere safe while I pay for my gas.

Oh—and put this on." He handed the boy his helmet as he strode toward the office, where he slapped down the money, not bothering to wait for change when nobody appeared at the counter.

"But where are we going?" Charlie asked, waiting by the bike as Dare came striding back.

Dare settled himself across the seat. "Your house."

"Really?" Charlie's voice crackled with surprise as he climbed aboard. "Why would you want to do that?"

"Because I'm going to have a little talk with your brother-in-law," he said grimly, firing up the engine.

"About what?"

"About what constitutes a *real* apology—and how really sorry he may soon be for his behavior lately."

Charlie hesitated, then wrapped his arms gingerly around Dare's waist in a tentative gesture of trust. "Does that mean you're gonna clean his clock?" he asked hopefully.

"In a manner of speaking. Now, hold on." He hunkered down, cranked up the accelerator and sent the Harley shooting out of the service station.

The rain passed quickly. The storm clouds peeled away, leaving behind a sky streaked with pink, lavender and blue.

The sun was bright at Victoria's back as she trudged up the back steps and let herself in the kitchen door, a grocery bag clutched in her arms.

She set it down on the counter. She was tired. The long night and the storm of morning tears that had followed Dare's departure had taken their toll.

Yawning, she began to unload her groceries. A loaf of bread. A dozen cans of cat food. Several frozen dinners.

With a sigh, she picked up the last items to put in the ice-box, only to freeze when a slight movement crossed the edge of her vision.

She wasn't alone.

Her heart dropped to her knees. The cheerful sound of the neighborhood kids playing Red Rover out in the street vanished, drowned out by the roar of the blood in her ears.

"I was right the first time." The familiar voice came out of the shadows. "You need a keeper. When are you going to learn to lock your doors?"

"Dare." She wasn't sure if she actually said his name or if it was only a cry torn from her heart. Emotion flooded her, making her weak in the knees. "What are you doing here?"

"I had a little talk with your friend Will Craig."

"You did?" She groped for the edge of the counter.

"Uh-huh. I told him he had a choice. He could see a counselor and get some help—or he could see a judge and get to know some prison guards. Guess which one he chose?"

She stared, dumbstruck, at his shadowed face. "Can—can you do that? I mean, won't you get in trouble—"

"I talked to my boss," he assured her. "It's not exactly by the book—but then, when have I ever played by the rules?" He took a step that carried him out of the darkness and into one of the stripes of sunshine that banded the floor. Light gilded him, shining in his inky hair, turning his eyes to liquid silver. "I talked to my boss about something else, Victoria. I told him I'd take that job at FLETC."

"You did?"

"Yeah. Except...I don't know one damn thing about teaching. I'm going to need help. I thought maybe you might be interested in taking me on."

Eyes riveted on his face, heart pounding, Victoria couldn't get a word around the lump in her throat.

"Before you answer, I suppose you ought to know there's a condition. We'd have to take Charlie with us—at least for a while. The Craigs are going to need some space to work things out and Charlie—well, Charlie needs some time to just be a kid."

Misunderstanding her silence, Dare played his trump card. "The thing is, I already know you prefer tea to coffee, peas to carrots and can't cook to save your life. And I rechecked the file, so I know your birthday's May twelfth. All those little things—" his voice broke "—and one big one. I know you love me, Victoria. And I love you."

"Oh, Dare..." Her eyes shiny with tears, Victoria walked across the room and into his arms.

For a long moment, Dare held her against him. Then he framed her face in his hands, no longer trying to hide how much she meant to him. It was there in his eyes, more brilliant than the sunshine that cloaked him. "I take it that's a yes?" Soft strands of her pale gold hair clung to his trembling fingers.

"*Yes.*"

"Then hold on for the adventure of your life, Teach," he said, "'cause I'm never letting you go."

"Promise?"

"It's a deal."

Just to make certain, they sealed it with a kiss.

*   *   *   *   *

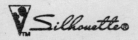

MILLION DOLLAR SWEEPSTAKES (III)

No purchase necessary. To enter, follow the directions published. Method of entry may vary. For eligibility, entries must be received no later than March 31, 1996. No liability is assumed for printing errors, lost, late or misdirected entries. Odds of winning are determined by the number of eligible entries distributed and received. Prizewinners will be determined no later than June 30, 1996.

Sweepstakes open to residents of the U.S. (except Puerto Rico), Canada, Europe and Taiwan who are 18 years of age or older. All applicable laws and regulations apply. Sweepstakes offer void wherever prohibited by law. Values of all prizes are in U.S. currency. This sweepstakes is presented by Torstar Corp., its subsidiaries and affiliates, in conjunction with book, merchandise and/or product offerings. For a copy of the Official Rules send a self-addressed, stamped envelope (WA residents need not affix return postage) to: MILLION DOLLAR SWEEPSTAKES (III) Rules, P.O. Box 4573, Blair, NE 68009, USA.

EXTRA BONUS PRIZE DRAWING

No purchase necessary. The Extra Bonus Prize will be awarded in a random drawing to be conducted no later than 5/30/96 from among all entries received. To qualify, entries must be received by 3/31/96 and comply with published directions. Drawing open to residents of the U.S. (except Puerto Rico), Canada, Europe and Taiwan who are 18 years of age or older. All applicable laws and regulations apply; offer void wherever prohibited by law. Odds of winning are dependent upon number of eligible entries received. Prize is valued in U.S. currency. The offer is presented by Torstar Corp., its subsidiaries and affiliates in conjunction with book, merchandise and/or product offering. For a copy of the Official Rules governing this sweepstakes, send a self-addressed, stamped envelope (WA residents need not affix return postage) to: Extra Bonus Prize Drawing Rules, P.O. Box 4590, Blair, NE 68009, USA.

SWP-S295

is

DIANA PALMER'S
THAT BURKE MAN

He's rugged, lean and determined. He's a
Long, Tall Texan. His name is Burke, and he's
March's *Man of the Month*—Silhouette Desire's
75th!

**Meet this sexy cowboy in Diana Palmer's
THAT BURKE MAN, available in March 1995!**

Man of the Month...only from Silhouette Desire!

DP75MOM

SILHOUETTE®

Desire®

MAN

of the

Month

1995

Don't let the winter months get
you down because the heat is
about to get turned way up...with
the sexiest hunks of 1995!

January: *A NUISANCE*
           by Lass Small

February: *COWBOYS DON'T CRY*
           by Anne McAllister

March: *THAT BURKE MAN*
           the 75th Man of the Month
           by Diana Palmer

April: *MR. EASY*
           by Cait London

May: *MYSTERIOUS MOUNTAIN MAN*
           by Annette Broadrick

June: *SINGLE DAD*
           by Jennifer Greene

           MAN OF THE MONTH...
           ONLY FROM
           SILHOUETTE DESIRE

MOM95JJ-R

A new series from Nancy Martin

Who says opposites don't attract?

Three sexy bachelors
should've seen trouble coming
when each meets a woman
who makes his blood boil—
and not just because she's beautiful....

In March—
THE PAUPER AND THE PREGNANT PRINCESS (#916)

In May—
THE COP AND THE CHORUS GIRL (#927)

In September—
THE COWBOY AND THE CALENDAR GIRL

Watch the sparks fly as these handsome hunks fall for
the women they swore they didn't want!
Only from Silhouette Desire.

Robert...Luke...Noah
Three proud, strong brothers who live—and
love—by

THE CODE OF THE WEST

Meet the Tanner man, starting with
Silhouette Desire's *Man of the Month* for
February, Robert Tanner, in Anne McAllister's

COWBOYS DON'T CRY

Robert Tanner never let any woman get close
to him—especially not Maggie MacLeod. But
the tempting new owner of his ranch was
determined to get past the well-built defenses
around his heart....

And be sure to watch for brothers Luke and Noah,
in their own stories, COWBOYS DON'T QUIT
and COWBOYS DON'T STAY, throughout 1995!

Only from

SILHOUETTE® *Desire*®

SILHOUETTE... Where Passion Lives

Don't miss these Silhouette favorites by some of our most distinguished authors! And now you can receive a discount by ordering two or more titles!

SD#05786	QUICKSAND by Jennifer Greene	$2.89	☐
SD#05795	DEREK by Leslie Guccione	$2.99	☐
SD#05818	NOT JUST ANOTHER PERFECT WIFE		
	by Robin Elliott	$2.99	☐
IM#07505	HELL ON WHEELS by Naomi Horton	$3.50	☐
IM#07514	FIRE ON THE MOUNTAIN		
	by Marion Smith Collins	$3.50	☐
IM#07559	KEEPER by Patricia Gardner Evans	$3.50	☐
SSE#09879	LOVING AND GIVING by Gina Ferris	$3.50	☐
SSE#09892	BABY IN THE MIDDLE	$3.50 U.S.	☐
	by Marie Ferrarella	$3.99 CAN.	☐
SSE#09902	SEDUCED BY INNOCENCE	$3.50 U.S.	☐
	by Lucy Gordon	$3.99 CAN.	☐
SR#08952	INSTANT FATHER by Lucy Gordon	$2.75	☐
SR#08984	AUNT CONNIE'S WEDDING		
	by Marie Ferrarella	$2.75	☐
SR#08990	JILTED by Joleen Daniels	$2.75	☐

(limited quantities available on certain titles)

AMOUNT	$_____
DEDUCT: 10% DISCOUNT FOR 2+ BOOKS	$_____
POSTAGE & HANDLING	$_____
($1.00 for one book, 50¢ for each additional)	
APPLICABLE TAXES*	$_____
TOTAL PAYABLE	$_____
(check or money order—please do not send cash)	

To order, complete this form and send it, along with a check or money order for the total above, payable to Silhouette Books, to: **In the U.S.**: 3010 Walden Avenue, P.O. Box 9077, Buffalo, NY 14269-9077; **In Canada**: P.O. Box 636, Fort Erie, Ontario, L2A 5X3.

Name:_____

Address:_____ City:_____

State/Prov.:_____ Zip/Postal Code:_____

*New York residents remit applicable sales taxes.
Canadian residents remit applicable GST and provincial taxes.   SBACK-DF

Silhouette®